THE TWICE-LIVED SUMMER OF BLUEBELL JONES

Susie Day grew up in Penarth, Wales, with a lisp and a really unfortunate first name. Her many careers have included guiding tourists, professional nappy-changing, teaching small people how many beans make five and taller people how to interrogate the beans from a post-structuralist perspective, and herding boarding school students – but she always wanted to be a writer. She firmly believes in the dictum "write what you know", which is why this book is about time-travel, love, and regrettable shoes. Susie lives in Oxford, and is probably drinking a cup of tea right now (she usually has one around this time of day).

THE TWICE-LIVED SUMMER OF BLUEBELL JONES

SUSIE DAY

First published in the UK in 2012 by Marion Lloyd Books
An imprint of Scholastic Children's Books
Euston House, 24 Eversholt Street
London, NW1 1DB, UK
Registered office: Westfield Road, Southam, Warwickshire, CV47 0RA
SCHOLASTIC and associated logos are trademarks and/
or registered trademarks of Scholastic Inc.

ISBN 978 1407 12084 3

A CIP catalogue record for this book is available
from the British Library

Printed and bound by CPI Group (UK) Ltd, Croydon CR0 4YY

1 3 5 7 9 10 8 6 4 2

www.scholastic.co.uk/zone

For Tania, Leo and Angelica, and for Nick

CONTENTS

1. HAPPY BIRTHDAY, BLUEBELL JONES

I'm carrying my birthday cake through Penkerry fairground when I hear the first scream.

There's screaming all around me, obviously. It trails above my head as the Whirler Twirler spins, fighting with chopped-up old pop songs. It crashes through the doors of the Ghost Train. Penkerry people like being frightened. Now I'm thirteen, I expect I'll start to like being flung in the air and shaken till I'm sick, too: the tacky lights, and that fried onion smell. I don't yet. Maybe it takes a few days to kick in.

Those are happy screams, though. This one is pure panic.

There's another. And another.

The bright lights keep flashing, the waltzers keep spinning – but it feels like everything stops. Everyone turns. And then I see it: the Red Dragon roller coaster, Penkerry's number one attraction (it says in my *Top Ten Things To See and Do* leaflet from the Tourist Information). Twelve scaly red cars, with a spiked tail and an evil fanged head. Its eyes burn yellow. It pumps out clouds of smoke. It flies round the highest three hundred and sixty degree loop in all of Wales, and its party trick is to stop, at the peak of the loop, and hang the riders upside-down while a plume of flame shoots into the air. Wales's ultimate thrill-ride.

It's stuck. Upside-down, in the very centre of the loop. The flames have shot up, screams earned. But instead of flying on down the tracks, it's stopped.

I can see a girl's loose hair hanging down, framed against the cloudy grey of the sky. One mad boy is letting his arms dangle. Everyone else is clinging on to the safety bars across their chests, and screaming, and screaming.

"They're going to fall, oh my god, they're going to fall!" breathes a woman on to my shoulder, as the crowd I'm suddenly in surges closer, all elbows.

No, they won't, I think, clutching my cake box tighter. There are rules to stop that. Safety precautions. The world doesn't let dodgy-looking boys with invisible moustaches take your three quid and send you breathing fire a hundred metres high and upside-down without there being rules. The world wouldn't let that happen. Not on my birthday.

The lights go out. Not across the rest of the fair – but the Red Dragon goes dark. First the booth, then slowly all along the tracks by sections: off, off, off. Then the Dragon itself; mean yellow eyes burnt out to black.

I can smell petrol.

I keep on thinking, it's OK, it must be all right – but there's a new scream piercing the air, impossibly high, and I see her.

The girl with the dangling hair is trying to climb out.

That's why there are rules: she's too small, too young, there's a "Taller Than Me To Ride!" sign at the gates, but no one's checked her and she isn't – I can see that from here – she's a slippery little eel person of six or seven, popping her narrow shoulders out from under the U-shaped safety bar across her chest like soap in wet hands. There's someone bigger in the next-door seat – a man: dad, grandad maybe – and his arm is outstretched, trying frantically to block her in.

Her shoulders slither all the way out. Her hanging hair blows around her face. Knees still held fast under the other safety bar, she bends double and reaches up with both bare skinny arms towards the rails above. Like she's on monkey bars at a park. Like she doesn't understand the danger.

There's screaming, and screaming.

Hold on; no, no, please, please, don't. . .

One butter-yellow sandal drops off her foot, all the way down. I follow it with my eyes, and as I jolt my head back up, she slips.

She screams.

It's impossible, how time cheats. It waits long enough for us all to see her small hands clutch and catch nothing. It holds its breath as we watch, her scream one endless piping note.

The man – dad, grandad – clamps his arm across the seats and pins her in place.

He saves her.

He rescues her.

The lights flicker back on, one by one. Her other sandal topples to the ground, forgotten as the crowds cheer.

I drop my birthday cake on the ground, splat.

"Oi!" says Tiger, poking me with a hairbrush. "Stand still, will you? I've got to do mine yet."

Tiger draws long fat slugs of eyeliner above my lashes, with flicks at the end.

"You like?" she says, spinning me round in the tiny Pavilion bathroom so I face the mirror.

I look like her.

Well, ish. My big sister Tigerlily has white-blonde dreadlocks and the sort of blue eyes people write poems about. I know it's my birthday but still: it's eyeliner, not magic.

Tiger puts frosty pink lipstick on me in two quick sweeps, smoothes my fringe, then pushes me out of the bathroom for inspection.

"Bloody hell!" says Mum. "No, no, in a good way," she adds quickly, seeing my face. "You look. . ."

"Offensively cute," says Dad, peering in through the backstage curtains, "even if I am biased. Also shockingly grown up. In fact, go away, you're making me feel old."

"You are old, Mr Grey Hair," shouts Tiger from the bathroom.

"That's Mr Just For Men Espresso Coffee Deluxe, thank you," Dad shouts back, smoothing a hand over his shiny slicked-back quiff.

"Grey grows back, honey," says Mum. "You'd better get used to people calling you 'Grandad'."

She strokes her hand over her bump. Her stretched-out T-shirt says ROCK-A-HULA BABY with an arrow pointing to where Peanut is. That's my baby brother or sister in there, inside my mum. I've had six whole months to get used to the idea, and it's still creepy and horrifying.

Well, it was. Not now I'm thirteen. Thirteen-year-olds are comfortable with all forms of lady business.

Thirteen-year-olds are supposed to keep secrets from their parents, too.

I haven't told them about the girl on the Red Dragon. I don't know why. By the time I got here they'd heard the fire engines, the local gossip about who would be blamed and who should be sacked, and she was already a story: the little girl who didn't fall. They laughed when I opened the cardboard cake box and they saw the smeared blue icing. HA PU BIRT LAY BLUBL. Then Tiger was wrapping my fringe around a hot roller, and somehow there wasn't any time to say I was there too and I saw it happen and I was scared.

I'm being silly, anyway. It's my birthday, my big day. No reason to spoil it.

Dad starts tap-tap-tapping on the wall with Mum's drumsticks, impatient, excited.

There's a buzz outside. The main doors are open. Their audience is here.

It's opening night for the summer season, and *Joanie and the Whales* are the main attraction at the Penkerry Pier Pavilion. Mum is the band's founding member (she's Joanie, not a whale, as Dad likes to helpfully point out) and drummer – at least until Peanut decides she or he doesn't like being squashed in behind the drum kit any more. The others come and go: right now it's Janice on bass and Woody on keyboards. Dad's the frontman: vocals and guitar. They do rock'n'roll covers from the 1950s, rockabilly and a little swing, plus whatever the crowd in the pub or at the wedding reception yells for.

My parents aren't full-time rock stars; Mum says a fifties band doesn't pay the twenty-first-century bills. But they're both teachers, so this summer is theirs. They're going to play the Pavilion every Friday and Saturday night. They'll be the opening act for the Fifties Fest later in the summer, when apparently a bunch of retro obsessives flood Penkerry from all over the country, in ancient cars with fins, dressed up in dead people's clothes off eBay.

Dad's been fizzy with anticipation all day, like it's his birthday too. He grew up in Penkerry. Playing the Pavilion stage is sort of his lifetime ambition.

I can't spoil it. The little Red Dragon girl is fine. The man held her in until the power came back on – a minute, no more – and they rolled back down to earth. It didn't happen to me. I don't know why I'm thinking about it at all.

Dad tap-tap-taps the drumsticks again, and I dip into the guitar case stacked against the wall.

"Made you a present," I tell him, pressing a neatly printed page into his hands.

"A set-list!" he says. "And it's . . . laminated!"

"So you can reuse it all summer," I explain.

"Oh, baby girl, you are *so* rock'n'roll," Mum says, planting a big kiss on the top of my head.

The backstage lights flip on and off. It's show time.

"Happy birthday, sweetheart. This one's for you," says Dad with a wink, as he hands Mum her sticks and pulls her through the curtain.

Tiger tells me to stop fiddling with my ponytail, and drags me out through the back door. We run out into the drizzle and on to the pier, down the wet wooden planks of the narrow passageway alongside the Pavilion.

The tide's coming in. I can see the sea far below my feet, in the gaps between the planks.

My shoes are too big. My heels keep slipping out.

It smells like chips and candyfloss, salt and sick. Back on the shore, beyond the promenade, there's a POLICE INCIDENT sign propped on the pavement. The funfair is gloomy and dark, locked iron gates criss-crossed with strings of blue and white tape. No bright lights. No screams. No entry. It's getting late, but with the fair closed there's nowhere to go, so the beach is still dotted with families; kids with buckets and spades, even though the beach is made of pebbles not sand and that's just not practical.

We reach the front entrance of the Pavilion, right in the middle of the pier, and skid up the steps, back into the dark. It's like an old theatre inside, only with a dance floor instead of rows of chairs. The windowless walls are like one of those old-fashioned cinemas: fake marble pillars, golden angels. On the ceiling there's a glitter ball, throwing white loops across the angels' faces.

I can see Mum behind her drum kit, shouting something to Janice, laughing. Then there's a sudden hush. Out of the darkness a single spotlight flicks on: Dad, framed in white light on his stage. I can see this glow on his face as he straps on his guitar and steadies the mike. Like he knows, he just *knows*, that tonight will be everything he's ever hoped for.

I push the girl on the Red Dragon firmly to the back of my mind, and let it bubble up in me, too.

Birthday girl.

This is my moment. This is it. I've been watching thirteen happen to everyone else all year. The day Monique ordered plain black coffee, double shot, instead of frothy milk and vanilla syrup. Grace's pocket money transforming into a "monthly clothing allowance" to be spent on tiny dresses that show your pants. Being friends with boys, as if they're people.

Now it's my turn.

I know what everyone thinks of me. Boring Bluebell Jones: the shy girl with the practical ponytail who gets her homework in on time and never breaks the rules.

That girl's about to vanish. It's time for teenage Bluebell to come out to play. She is brave, and fabulous. She doesn't follow her friends meekly: she strikes out on her own, and they follow her. She's not afraid of anything, or anyone. She is the Very Hungry Caterpillar, she has eaten all her plums and her slices of salami, and tonight she's going to burst out of me like a beautiful butterfly.

I can't wait.

"Good evening, Penkerry," says Dad into the mike, his smile echoing into his voice. "We're Joanie and the Whales, and we're here to throw a party in the county jail."

He strums the first two chords, Mum whacks the drums twice like she's answering back: repeat, thrum thrum, whack whack, and they slam into "Jailhouse Rock".

No one's dancing. No one ever does at the start of a gig. But Tiger flings herself out on to the dance floor anyway, gradually sucking lurkers off the sidelines like a whirlpool.

I hesitate on the brink – then decide to wait this one out.

And the next. I can watch the band much better from the shadows, in the corner. And my shoes really are too big.

The men at the bar are all talking over the music, moaning about rain and beer in plastic cups. I ignore them and watch, taking imaginary photographs: the pretty elf girl with a nose ring and lots of silver bangles, joining Tiger on the dance floor, matching her moves; a huddle of people about my age, hanging around at the coat-check.

There's a Chinese girl wearing purple lace-up boots, a chubby guy in what looks like a pirate outfit, and a tall, skinny, eyelinered boy wearing a top hat with a dead red rose tucked into the brim. He's trying to look bored, but the girl with the lace-up boots is totally into the gig, singing along with a huge grin on her face, and she knows all the words.

I want to go over there. It's like I'm *supposed* to go over there: as if they're waiting for me.

It'll be easy.

I could ask her if her parents are weirdly obsessed with the 1950s too.

I could ask about the pirate outfit.

I could ask Top Hat Boy why he's wearing a top hat, or where the rose came from: confident, a little bit flirty; like Monique, like Grace.

I could just say, "Hi, my name's Bluebell, it's my birthday today."

But there's a lull between songs, and I hear *fairground* and *accident* from the voices at the bar.

Should close the whole bloody place down.

Nah, was the kid's own fault.

Me, I blame the parents, letting her on that thing in the first place.

A howl of feedback pours from the speakers, piercing like a scream. I stick my fingers in my ears. I clamp my eyes shut. The high-pitched whine drops out, and Joanie and the Whales kick into "Great Balls of Fire", the piano and the bass line rumbling through the floorboards – but I feel like I've been turned upside-down. It's as if I'm dangling high above, waiting to fall in the middle of the dance floor, splat.

That's when it hits me. This is what thirteen means: danger, change, the world turned upside-down. And it's scary, because I'm not a butterfly yet. I'm still a caterpillar girl, not big enough to ride the roller coaster.

Not ready to be thirteen at all.

No. That can't be right. There are rules; there have to be, even about birthdays.

I start to run – out of the Pavilion, back along the wet boards, into the safe warm shadows of backstage – not because I'm running away from anything; definitely not that. I need some air, some fresh air and to check my make-up (that's what teenage girls do, they do that loads, this is fine). Then I'm going straight back, and the butterfly will shoot right out of me. Somehow. Definitely.

My squashed white and blue cake is there on the dressing table.

HA PU BIRT LAY BLUBL, it says, sadly. Mum said we'd get a new one tomorrow, one that looks less like mashed potato, but she's already pushed in one skinny blue candle for me to blow out later.

There's a matchbox on the table, waiting.

It goes quiet onstage as I sink into a chair, wiping raindrops off my face. Then Dad's muffled crooning floats through the wall.

Every day, it's-a getting closer
Going faster than a roller coaster

I tap out the handclap-rhythm on the edge of the table, automatically. I've heard him sing this a thousand times. A cutesy little love song, sweet like sugar icing.

I look again at the candle, and the matchbox, and once the idea pops into my head I can't escape it. It's ridiculous. All I want is to be grown up, a real teenage girl, like Tiger, like Grace. But I don't feel thirteen yet, so why shouldn't I grab my chance to act like a little girl, one last time?

I fetch a big glass of water, because we've done the fire triangle at school and even wishes ought to be made in an appropriately safety-conscious environment. I fumble one match from the box and strike it (away from me, obviously). The shadow of my hand lunges huge and craggy, like a monster's, across the wall as I light the skinny candle. I stare into the flame, listening to Mum's drumbeats tapping. I shut my eyes tight, and whisper it:

I wish. . .

I have to get the words right.

I wish. . .

I think of the girl on the roller coaster; the girl who was saved.

I wish someone would rescue me.

There's a sighing sound, and my fringe ruffles like someone's opened a window.

Then someone *laughs*. It must be Tiger. Or maybe someone from the bar?

I scrabble for an unrelated-to-birthday-wishes excuse for me to be sitting in the dark in front of a candlelit cake with my eyes shut, but there aren't any, and the laughing happens again, so I crack open one eye.

It's not Tiger.

It's *me*. Brave hair. Fabulous grin. As different from me as possible. But it's undeniably me, another me, standing in the doorway with a daft excited look on my face.

"Happy birthday, Blue!" says the other me.

And she blows out my birthday candle.

2. RED

I run out of there so fast it doesn't matter that I'm wearing Tiger's shoes, or that under the planks of the pier is the sea, rumbling and hungry like those trolls under bridges in fairy stories.

Not that thirteen-year-olds believe in fairy stories. Thirteen-year-olds don't make birthday wishes and imagine they come true, either. I knew I shouldn't have eaten all those chips at lunchtime. Miss Kitchener says you aren't supposed to eat too many hydrogenated fats, and I bet they had loads. I've deep-fried my brain in poison, and this is the consequence.

I feel sick. And beyond pathetic. This time I really am running away: past the locked-up gates of the silent fairground; past Penkerry Dairy ice-cream café, the chippy (urgh), the bright lights of the Lucky Penny arcade.

By the time I've made it up the big hill to Penkerry Point Caravan Park, I'm soaked. I towel off, leaving behind slug-trails of mascara, and swap my stupid borrowed clingy skirt for pyjamas. I scoop my duvet off the top bunk, grabbing Milly the one-eyed mouse too. I expect proper thirteen-year-olds don't take a cuddly toy with them on holiday to help them sleep, but me and Milly don't care. We're going to curl up and watch crap TV on the sofa, just us. Maybe eat some biscuits.

"Oh yeah, you *really* know how to party," says a voice from the sofa.

Oh god. It's her again. Me. Only . . . *not*.

With a yelp, I throw the duvet at her and bolt for the bathroom, slamming the door. Then I run both taps and start brushing my teeth. And humming. Not for any particular reason. Definitely not because there's a shouty figment of my imagination on the other side of the door.

"Oi! Blue! You wished me here, you can't just bugger off!" she yells through the plywood.

She can't be me. I'm not at all shouty.

"Hellooooo? This is moderately freaky for me too, you know?"

The figment of my imagination seems to want me to sympathize with it.

"Blue? What are you doing in there? I hope you're not trying to get those black bits off that sink, 'cos trust me: never going to happen."

There are black stains on the sink. Tiger dyed Dad's hair this morning, after he had a panic attack about three curly white hairs interfering with his quiff. It dripped on the taps, and the shower curtain as well. We're going to get in loads of trouble for that: there's a sign in the caravan park office – £50 flat rate charge for damage to property.

How can anyone else know there are black hair-dye stains on our sink?

"Hello, Bluuuuu-e?"

I shout "Stop calling me Blue!" through the door. "No one calls me Blue. It's Bluebell. My name is Bluebell."

"You *hate* being called Bluebell!" the figment shouts. "And everyone calls you 'Blue' – or they will soon. It's cute. It's a nickname. Like everyone calls me 'Red'."

I have to open the bathroom door then, because I've been wondering about that.

My hair is mousey brown, with a fringe, the rest always neatly tied back.

Hers is red. Very red. London bus, traffic light, warning sign red. Short, too: cropped close above one ear and longer over the other, with a chin-length swoop of smooth hair like a parakeet's wing dangling over one eye. It's the sort of haircut I'd never have.

But that's my freckly face beaming behind it. Those are my feet, in those biker boots. Those are my arms, sticking out of an artistically scruffified purple T-shirt with a yellow smiley face on it. *My bum is in those denim cut-offs.*

"Yay!" she says. Out loud, like it's a word.

She can't possibly be me.

But I look in her eyes and behind the beam and the boots I can tell she's a little bit nervous, a little bit out of place. She's real. This is happening. I needed someone to rescue me, and here she is.

"It worked," I whisper. "I . . . I wished you here."

Red nods proudly. "Well, not just you all by yourself," she adds. "I mean, one wish on its own doesn't come true — otherwise when you were six you'd have blown out your birthday candles and Tiger would've turned into a talking pony called Pippi Clip-Clop, remember?"

Whoa. I've never told anyone that.

Red grins. "Don't worry, I'm as repulsed by our six-year-old self as you are."

"So, if I couldn't wish you here on my own. . ." I say slowly, trying to catch up. "That means you wished for it too? At the exact same time as me?"

She slips her hands into her pockets and shakes the wing of hair out of her eyes, giving me a flash of silver earrings (two! In one ear!). A steady smile creeps across her mouth.

"Yeah," she says, half-word, half-laugh. "I guess we must have."

"So is it your birthday as well? Your. . ." I look her up and down. "Fourteenth birthday?"

She looks down at herself, then at me.

"Yeah," she laughs again.

"You're from the *future*?"

"Yeah!"

I sit down on the closed lid of the toilet, hard. A tiny corner of my brain is thinking sensible, practical, this-is-scientifically-impossible thoughts. But the rest is froth made of questions. What's it like in the future? When will I cut my hair and turn into you? Is Grace still my Best Friend

Forever? Did you happen to write down this week's lottery numbers somewhere handy? Will I. . .

"Oh!" My voice is squeaky as I clap my hands to my lips. "Do I have a baby brother or a baby sister?"

Red takes a breath, and opens her mouth to answer – but suddenly outside I hear someone singing "Girl, You'll Be A Woman Soon" in a fake cowboy accent, and a lot of noisy shushing.

Red's mouth clamps shut.

She jerks a thumb towards the noise. "Is that. . .?" she whispers.

"Yes! Go! You've got to go!" I yelp, leaping out of the tiny bathroom towards the caravan's front door.

The key scrapes in the lock.

"Go where?" says Red, looking round. "It's a caravan! And that's the only door!"

"The bedroom!" I hiss, pushing the front door closed again as it begins to swing inwards. "Hide in the bedroom!"

The caravan has two: one with a double bed for Mum and Dad next to the bathroom, and mine and Tiger's narrow one alongside it, with bunk beds and a scratchy orange curtain instead of a door.

"Oi, you weirdo!" shouts Tiger yawnily, hammering from outside. "Tired people getting rained on out here!"

"Just a minute!"

I glance over my shoulder. No sign of Red, just a flapping orange curtain.

Phew.

"Hi!" I say, pulling the door inwards, stepping back to

18

let Mum, Dad and Tiger in, and casually resting an elbow on the wall so I'm blocking the corridor. "How are you? How is . . . everything?"

"Er, we're fine. You, I'm suddenly not so sure about," says Tiger, giving me a stare as she hefts Dad's guitar case on to the sofa.

"Two encores, birthday girl!" says Dad, trying to give me a victory hug even though he's soaking wet.

"The second one was to a totally empty room, but then that's never stopped him before," says Mum, shaking drips off the tips of her hair. "You feeling all right, baby? We were worried when we couldn't find you."

"Sorry. I'm fine." I glance back at the orange curtain. "I mean, I felt a bit sicky, earlier, so I left. I should probably go and lie down. In the quiet. On my own."

"You crash out, petal," Dad says. "I'll bring you in some tea, settle your tum."

"No!" It comes out louder than I mean, and he raises an eyebrow. "Don't bother. I'm going to go straight to sleep."

Tiger yawns, and tries to slide past me. I slap my palm flat against the sticky wood-effect vinyl on the wall, blocking her path.

"Hey! I'm just going to change, so I don't wake you up crashing around when I go to bed, OK?"

She grabs my wrist and pushes, and I shuffle backwards along the narrow passage, still trying to block her, right up to the orange curtain.

Tiger crinkles her perfect forehead and narrows her big blue eyes. "What did you do? Did you break something?

Lose something? If you've spilled that grim bluebell perfume all over my bed. . ."

I shake my head.

"Well, what then?"

I swallow, hard. Before I can find the right words, Tiger raises both eyebrows sky-high.

"Have you got a *boy* in there?" she whispers, sounding both thunderstruck and utterly thrilled.

Dad's head snaps round. "What? What was that?" His head plonks on to Tiger's shoulder, mouth cartoon-wide. "Really, has she got a boy in there?"

They exchange gleeful grins.

Honestly, with role models like these it is a miracle that I even exist.

"No!" I hiss – and then Dad tickles my side so my arm drops, and Tiger ducks round me to swish the curtain open.

I squeeze my eyes tight shut.

"What's he like?" shouts Mum from the sofa.

"Skinny," Dad shouts back.

I open my eyes, half-expecting to find that a skinny boy has somehow decided to appear out of my imagination too.

But there's no boy.

No Red, either.

Tiger checks under the bed and in the narrow wardrobe and, well, there are no other hiding places because, like Red said, it's a caravan.

Except there is no Red.

Of course there's no Red. There's just stupid old me:

Bluebell Jones, who is so pathetically still a child that she's made up an imaginary friend.

Dad slips his hand under my fringe to feel for a temperature, and crinkles his brow seriously. "Yep, there's no doubt. Skin, then some kind of bony structure, like a skull, and inside?" He raps my forehead. "The mysterious brain of a teenage girl."

I wish.

I dream that Mum has the baby, and it is a literal peanut. She wheels it around in a pram, and takes it on funfair rides, as if it is a normal-sized normal-shaped baby with a face and arms and legs, and no one says a word.

I like it. It's quiet, and doesn't take up space.

I wake up with Milly the mouse's worn ear pressed against my cheek, and a clanging twisting feeling, like I've done something bad. Forgotten-PE-kit bad. Argument-with-Grace, everyone-hates-me bad.

Then I remember. It was my birthday yesterday, and I thought I saw another me. A grown-up, brilliant, teenage me.

All in my head. Nothing's changed at all. Why didn't Grace tell me thirteen isn't just a thing that happens to you overnight, without you having to do anything?

Why didn't I work it out myself? I'm brainy. I got As in Science and Maths and DT and Art and a B in English even though Miss Kitchener says I need to take a less literal attitude towards poetry. (I don't, though. Poetry is stupid. If you think someone is nice you can just tell them they're nice, you don't have to go on and on about how their hair is like a tinkling stream and put "O!" at the beginning of all your sentences.)

But I'm not *just* brainy. I know I'm not bright and shiny like Dad or Tiger or Mum, but I'm not terrible. I have interests. I have extra-curricular leisure pursuits. I like Pixar films and Parma Violets. I am gradually wallpapering the entire surface of my bedroom with perfectly tessellating photographs; one wall's half done already, and, in patchwork, a corner of the slopey ceiling over my bed. I wake up every day to see the same two pictures: me and Grace poking out our tongues, and a close-up of Tiger's left eye, huge like a wet pebble. When I grow up I would like to find a cure for peanut allergy, and take pictures for magazines.

And there's all the rest. I'm bigger on the inside. I worry about the future and exams and university fees and jobs and, you know, dolphins in tuna nets. And who I'll be, and why. I've been the boring parts of a teenager for years already. I've just been waiting for my outsides to catch up, so everyone else can see it.

But last night, it didn't happen. And I don't know how to fix it.

I make a little moany noise of misery, then clamp Milly

to my mouth. Tiger's not normally visible to the human eye before ten; wake her any earlier and she's all snarls.

I roll over and hang my head off the bunk to check, wrinkling my nose at the flotsam of books and clothes she's managed to spread over the tiny floor space already. It's AS level results day in four weeks. From the number of books, I think she's planning a few resits. I don't need a ladder to get down from the top bunk; I could fashion my own out of Cliffs Notes and knickers.

(All my stuff should be on the floor too. Thirteen-year-olds are messy. Why am I not suddenly uncharacteristically messy?)

Tiger's not there. I can see the covers have been slept in, but she's gone. I look at my watch: half past seven. Maybe Penkerry makes everyone go peculiar.

I toss and turn in the narrow bunk for a bit, but Dad's snores keep thrumming through the cardboard wall. Eventually I give up on sleeping, flip over, and tug out the bag that's wedged behind my pillow.

My birthday presents. They don't exactly cheer me up. Tiger got me Haribo, and a clockwork mouse for the Great Mouse Army that lives on my bookshelves at home. Mum and Dad got me a camera, like they promised. All mine, so I don't have to keep begging to borrow Mum's digital.

This one's called a Diana, and it's new but made to look old: plasticky, junk-shoppy. It's got a huge squarish flash that snaps on to the top, like an old cartoon. It even uses film, so there's no screen to see the picture you just took –

and the prints are supposed to come out ultra-bright and unreal, like *The Wizard of Oz*.

Thirteen-year-old me should find that vintagey and hipster.

I just wish they'd got me something they thought *I* might like.

As for the rest of the pressie pile – from all the uncles, and Granny in Australia, even Grace – it follows the usual theme. Bluebell notelets. Bluebell soap. Perfume that smells like bluebells, with a plastic bluebell wedged in the bottle. Tiger never gets old-lady-smelling stuff for her birthdays. I don't think they make stuff with tiger lilies on. Or tigers. Even if they did it would be all fierce and grr and Tigerish. I'd wear perfume if it smelled like tigers and had a plastic tiger in it.

We've got a list of possible Peanut names pinned up on the fridge, brought from home. I should be a kind future big sister and swap out all the stupid flowery names for better present inspiration. Like "Money", or "iPod". "Giftcard" has a nice ring to it. *Meet my baby brother/sister, Giftcard Jones.* That way Peanut will never, ever have a birthday as rubbish as this one.

There are scrunchy footsteps on the gravel outside, and a click at the door. A moment later, Tiger appears, flushed and sweaty. She's wearing jog bottoms and too-white trainers, and there's a twinkly smile in her eyes as she swishes through the orange curtain.

"Morning!" she announces, then bites her lip, guiltily dropping her voice to a whisper. "You should get up, it's gorgeous out there!"

24

"Where have you been?" I whisper back.

"For a run on the beach," she says brightly.

I don't think I've even seen Tiger run for a bus.

She tugs off her trainers, still laced up, and swishes back through the curtain. I hear the plasticky throb of water hitting the base of the shower, and her singing to herself through the wall.

I bet the pretty nose-ringed elf girl goes for a morning run on the beach too. Tiger's only just stopped sobbing herself to sleep over breaking up with Sasha the Cow (even though she was a cow), but Tiger goes through girlfriends like Dad does guitar strings. Looks like she's back in the game.

People always ask what it's like, having a sister who goes out with girls. Like they think it's catching.

Seriously. Yesterday I was twelve. I'm sharing my bed with a cuddly mouse. I don't think I even have a sexuality to be confused about yet.

I suppose I should start worrying about that now, too.

I stare at Milly's single orange eye. It stares back, accusingly, as if even she thinks I should've outgrown her.

I throw her on the floor in disgust.

"Whoa, there! Don't take it out on the mouse."

I scrunch my eyes up tight, but it's not like I don't recognize the voice.

"Morning!" says Red. She's standing there, right next to my bunk bed. Same smiley-face T-shirt and cut-off shorts. Same wicked grin. Same total-impossibleness.

"Yes, I'm really here, no, you aren't dreaming or mental,

I really am you from the future, and *please* can we skip all this part because, hello, everyone hates that bit in a film where the hero is stupid and needs the whole plot explained to them even though it was all written on the back of the DVD."

I blink at her from behind a safe corner of my pillow. "Am I really seeing you? How did you get in? Where did you go last night?" My stomach does a backflip, and I wield the pillow between us like a shield, pressing myself against the wall, as far back as I can get. "Were you here all night and I just couldn't see you? Or am I just, you know . . . insane and seeing things?"

Red's shoulders flop. "Seriously, we have to do all this?"

There's a hammering on the cardboardy wall, as the shower noise cuts off.

"Oi! Keep it down in there!" shouts Mum. Her voice is muffled, but not much; she can probably hear everything in here just as clearly.

I clap my hand over my mouth.

Red smirks, unhelpfully.

"Sorry!" I call through the wall. "I'm. . ." My eyes scan the mess on the floor. "Just reading one of Tiger's books. Out loud."

"*Very* convincing," says Red.

"Shhh, she'll hear you!"

"What?" shouts Mum.

"Nothing!" I shout, as Red goes on smirking. "Wait – she *can't* hear you?" I say, this time super-soft.

"You think?"

26

I press my lips very firmly together.

Red rolls her eyes. "Look, we can't talk in here. And what're you doing still in bed anyway? There's the whole of Penkerry out there and you're sat in your jammies. Get dressed, meet me on the cliff top."

The shower door slides open again.

"Red – she's coming – how will you get—" I squeak, in a panic, as Red shows no sign of moving.

"Wha?" grunts Tiger, swishing through the orange curtain wrapped in a towel, dreadlocks all piled in a knot on top of her head.

"Ohhh," I breathe, my eyes going wide as Red gives me a flash of a grin. Tiger can't see Red. Only me, talking to myself. Then Red walks backwards through the wall. Straight through it, leaving nothing behind but a wisp of smoke like a blown candle.

I know the caravan walls are cardboard-thin, but that is still quite unexpected.

My fourteen-year-old self has amazing hair and walks through walls. I like me more already.

3. A GIRL WHO STANDS ON CLIFF EDGES

I take a ten-second shower, fling on the top layer of clothes from my suitcase, and brush my dampish hair back into its usual ponytail. Then I hesitate, and stroke one hand up the back of my neck. It tingles. I shake the ponytail, feeling it swish. What will it feel like, when I've cut that hair off? I can't wait to ask.

Dad has other ideas. By the time I'm dressed, he's filling the kitchenette with burnt toast and bacon smells, squeezing out teabags with his fingertips. Tiger's already sitting at the table, gazing fondly at the ketchup bottle.

"Not officially a holiday till you've had a bacon sarnie for breakfast," Dad says, and he looks so pleased with himself, waving his spatula about, that I can't just leave.

"So what's on the itinerary today, baby?" asks Mum, sleepily padding out to join us, her dressing gown knotted

28

but not quite meeting in the middle. "Are we going anywhere nice?"

Dad flips open the diary I've made, stuffed with printed maps off the internet and little notes in my round handwriting. We're here for six weeks, and I've planned the whole of our first one: bird sanctuary, chocolate factory, boat trip out to Mulvey Island lighthouse. All the essentials from the *Penkerry and Surrounding Area Top Ten Fun Attractions for all the Family*.

It looks stupid now.

"Dearie me, I think Bluebell might have to learn a bit of flexibility," says Dad, eyeing the diary. "Doesn't say anything in here about testing out any of your birthday presents. . ."

I might learn to love my weird plasticky new camera after all.

Half an hour later I'm running out of the caravan with Diana tucked in my bag, leaving Mum and Dad throwing each other proud looks about how much they nailed my birthday present.

I weave through the other caravans, past the row of posh chalets with sea views, across the grass. Clumps of bushes mark the edge of the cliffs, with a spindly iron fence blocking the sheer drop. In places the fence leans out, almost level with the ground, as if someone's already leant on it and fallen off. It's probably illegal. Red doesn't care, though. She's standing on the edge, breathing in salt.

She's me. I wished her here, and she's real (in a walking-through-walls kind of way) and when I grow up I'm going to be *her*. A girl who stands on cliff edges. Red, not Blue.

I wipe bacony hands on my jeans, squint through Diana's tiny viewfinder, and click a shot off quickly. Red poses at once, arms flexed like a weightlifter, as if she *likes* having her picture taken.

"It won't come out, you know," she laughs. "I can walk through furniture, I'll slide right off camera film."

She's probably right. I can't help trying to pin her into a picture, though.

The film needs to be wound on after each shot, and there's this funny system for taking different-sized prints, and a button for daylight versus night shots, and I wish it wasn't so obvious that I'm only fussing about with Diana because I don't have a clue what to say. I thought she'd feel familiar, equal. But Red's like a celebrity, or a superhero; bigger than life.

I so want her to like me. She grins, as if she knows *exactly* what I'm thinking – because she probably does. It doesn't help.

"Oh!" I squeak, suddenly even more embarrassed. "I forgot to say: happy birthday. For yesterday, I mean."

Red's smile gets even bigger. "Bless, get you with the lovely manners. I'm so nice! I didn't know I was that nice. Oh my god, are you wearing those shoes? I'd forgotten them. They're disgusting; I can't believe I ever went out in public with them on. Whoa: apparently I'm not nice any more, I'm patronizing and rude. Sorry. Really. That's . . . sorry."

Her red hair blows about her stricken face in the cliff-top wind, and I can see she's trying to be kind. My shoes probably are disgusting: flat canvas lace-ups with blotchy pink and green flowers on them. "Don't worry about it, it's fine," I say.

"See?" she says. "So nice!"

Also, she has boobs. Not that I'm staring. But there are actual boobs, attached to my body which has my face on it. Me, I only have flat bits and fat bits. Tiger's the one who overflows in all the right places. I'd given up waiting for them to pop up, and now, there they are. Boobs are in my future.

I might be staring.

Does she know what I'm thinking? Is that why she's smiling? Why am I still thinking about boobs? Boobs boobs boobs.

"Why are you here?" I blurt.

Her hopeful smile fades a touch. I'm ruining it already. No wonder lately Grace is always already out with Monique or Jen or some boy when I text her on Saturday mornings. I can't even talk to myself and not mess it up.

"That came out wrong! What I meant was . . . don't you have somewhere else to be? I mean – it's obvious why I made a wish. I need help. I need someone to rescue me from . . . me. But, well, look at you. You did it. You've done the growing-up thing. You're. . ."

I scrabble for the right words. Perfect? Incredible? OK, now I sound like a stalker. Girls aren't supposed to like themselves: it says so in Grace's magazines. Am I allowed to like me when I'm her?

"You're . . . fine," I stutter, eventually. "Better than fine.

Why would you wish yourself out of your own life, back to here?"

"It's Penkerry! Who wouldn't want to be here?" Red beams, flinging out an arm across the bay.

This is awkward. I see a dishwater sea, wafting the smell of decaying seaweed up my nose. Far-off pebbles dotted with tiny people pretending to sunbathe while rocks poke their backs and the sun fails to shine. The rusty pier. The fairground. The Red Dragon, a dark twist of iron against the sky.

She sees heaven.

"Haha, don't you love it!" Red picks up her shoulders and does a little run on the spot, like she just can't keep still. Then she catches my eye. "Well, OK, you don't love it yet. But you will. I guarantee it. And I'd know, right?"

She claps her hands, disappears into the clump of bushes right on the edge of the cliff, and vanishes.

She can walk through walls. Can she fly, too?

Then her perky red head reappears, peering through the bushes. "Short cut to the beach," she says, beckoning. "Come on. You've got new best friends to meet!"

For a second I feel sick. Tiger got all the small-talk genes in my family; round new people, I go shy and tongue-tied. But if they're her friends, they're going to like me too. Like she said: guaranteed.

I edge closer to the bushes, looking anxiously for the exact edge of the cliff, eyeing the bent iron railings warily. I have to take a step out into nothing to follow her – but my foot hits solid ground, and as I push through the prickly twigs, I can see it: a sandy windy yellow path, lined with green, sloping along the cliffs down to the beach.

I'd never have found it without her.

Penkerry is an attractive resort town, with a mile of pebble beach sheltered between two high cliffs, Verney Head and Penkerry Point, it says in my Tourist Information leaflet. *Picturesque Edwardian villas overlook the semicircular bay, accessed by a series of steeply winding narrow streets. The fairground is conveniently situated on the seafront, a few minutes' walk from the Victorian pier. Visitors can enjoy a boat trip to Mulvey Island lighthouse, sample the local Penkerry Dairy Ice Cream (seventeen flavours, including Raspberry Ripple, Candyfloss, and the unique Chilli Prawn – do you dare?), or relax in a deckchair on the prom. Fun for all the family!*

What the leaflet doesn't say: Penkerry is loud and smells of poo.

The cliff path leads us straight on to the promenade, the shop-lined road that runs the length of the beach. Babies wail. In the penny arcades, a million fruit machines go blipblipblipblipblip, not quite at the same time. People are eating chips at ten in the morning, and none of them seem to mind the cat-sized seagulls of death swooping at their faces making *argh argh* noises and trying to eat their children.

But Red is practically skipping, pointing out Frisky's

Mussel Hut, Deckchair Jim, giggling maniacally at The Bench – which is a bench. Just a bench. But we have to sit on it because apparently it's brilliant and amazing and I'll understand soon.

I try to see it through her eyes. Grace has gone to Bali for three weeks, whale-watching, and I don't know how a bench is going to compete with that. But that's why I wished her here. She can see what I can't.

"So, last night: where *did* you go?"

"I was right here," Red says. She moves to tap the wood of the bench, but her hand sinks into it palm-deep, the fingers disappearing in a puffy cloud of smoke. She gasps. "Brrr," she whispers, twisting her wrist and shivering as the smokiness swirls and slowly forms back into bone and flesh and skin. "I am *never* going to get used to that."

Me neither. I'm getting used to seeing her beside me, solid as I am. Watching bits of her vanish is terrifying.

"Hey, don't look so freaked out!" she says. "It doesn't hurt. I don't think I can get hurt, exactly." She frowns, as if she's trying to work out the rules for herself, too. I like that. It makes me feel like I'm the clever one, knowing there are some things even she isn't sure of.

"Can you sleep?"

"Don't need to." She shrugs. "That's good, though," she adds, gazing dreamily out across the water. "Penkerry's beautiful in the dark. I mean, I love it when it's all busy and mental and full of happy holiday people, but when it's quiet, it's like magic. They leave the pier lights on all night, and you can watch them dancing on the water. All you can hear is the crashing of the waves, the tide coming in, or the tide going out. It never stays still, never stops, and you can't argue with it. Can't fight it. It does what it wants. And then slowly, ever so slowly, the sun starts to come up, and the sky glows orange, and all these early-morning people come out and scuttle about like crabs, putting it ready for the day. I never saw that, when I was here last summer. You should sneak out and come with me, one night. I don't want you to miss it."

My toes tingle inside my dorky shoes. I'm going to be the kind of girl who stays out all night to watch sunrises. It's just so . . . *Tiger*. I sneak a sideways glance at Red, and she glows; almost pretty, and I never think that about me.

I might not love Penkerry yet, but I love knowing that I'm going to.

"Didn't you get cold?" I ask, looking at her thin purple T-shirt.

She barks with laughter. "All the questions in the universe, and that's what you want to know?"

It isn't. I could drown her in questions. What's it like, being a person made of candle smoke and wishes? Do you know already that's what I want to ask? Are you hungry? Are you tired? Does time feel long or short or exactly the same? Do you mind, that you're here not there?

And about the rest of this year she's already lived, too. Will I cry when I get my ears pierced? Does Grace like my hair? Are we still friends?

Did something happen, something big, to make me turn from Blue to Red?

"Oh!" I can't believe I forgot the most important question of all. Again. I am going to be a terrible big sister. "Peanut! Tell me about Peanut! Boy or girl? Did they call it something stupid? Please tell me it's not called Milk-Thistle?"

The list of potential baby names pinned on to the fridge is horrifying. There are some sensible ones – Rowan for a boy, and lots of girl ones, Poppy, and Rose (which I've crossed out and changed to Rosie, because it's nicer for a baby). I think Milk-Thistle and Hydrangea and Hedge are Dad just mucking about, but he did call me Bluebell; with him you can never be sure.

Until now, I suppose.

"Yeah," says Red, clearing her throat awkwardly. "About Peanut."

An awful, hollow bowl of dread appears in my stomach.

"No, don't panic, it's nothing bad!" Red looks mortified. "It's fine. Everyone's fine."

The bowl feeling goes away, just about. "Well?"

Red gives me a meaningful look, and taps the side of her nose three times, tap-tap-tap.

"What does that mean?"

"It means I'm not telling."

"What?"

"Sorry!" She doesn't look sorry. "It should be a surprise!" She grins. "I've been thinking about it all night. You're rubbish at keeping secrets: you'd be bound to let it slip. Anyway, no one should know too much about their own future. Where's the fun in life if you know exactly what's going to happen next?"

I curl my fingers under the edge of the bench, feeling the warm solid wood beneath me; gripping on tight. I don't understand. *Everyone* wants to know what happens next. If Tiger could get the letter with her exam results right this second instead of having to worry for another four weeks, of course she'd open it. If that little girl on the Red Dragon had known it would get stuck, of course she'd never have climbed on board.

"But. But that's why I wished you here. To rescue me from doing it all wrong."

"That's what *you* wished for," Red says, sitting back and crossing her boots. She squints into the far distance, along the promenade. Something – someone? – catches her eye, and the ghost of a twinkly smile appears in her eyes. "Doesn't mean I have to agree."

"What? But you have to help me!" I need her. I need to know when to cut my hair, where to buy those boots, how to be Red. How can she not get this?

Red throws me a pitying look. "Didn't say I wouldn't help." She gazes intently into the distance again, over my shoulder. "Maybe I'm here to rescue you from yourself. You don't always need a carefully planned itinerary, Blue. That's what really needs to change. Life's no fun without surprises. Ignore all the maps and timetables and Top Ten lists. Your future will find you. Trust me. If you relax, sit back – it might just walk right up and introduce itself."

She flashes me a grin and hops off The Bench, leaving three-quarters of it empty – just in time for a girl to sit down in her place.

"Hiya," says the girl, in a thick Welsh accent just like Dad's. "Excuse my feet, these boots are killing." And she starts to unlace her purple boots, right there on the bench, till her socks are off and her sore pink toes are wiggling in the fresh air.

I politely look the other way. I wouldn't want some total stranger staring at my blisters.

"Didn't I see you last night, down the Pav?" she says, lighting a cigarette.

Purple boots. It's the Chinese girl who knew all the words. And here she is, red heart-shaped sunglasses perched on her nose, roll-up burning between her fingers, chatting away like she doesn't mind my dorky flowery shoes, or my ponytail, or the way I must have spent the last five minutes talking to myself on a bench. Like we're already mates.

The girl yawns and stretches, arms up, neck arching back so her hair hangs over the back of the bench, feet off the ground with starfish toes. She's wearing a checked shirt, tied in a knot at the front, and it rides up so there's a bit of tummy showing: a little bit of pudge and hip overflowing her cropped jeans. But she doesn't pull her top down to cover it, like I would. She's busy. She's comfy. This is my bench, the bit of pudge seems to say. I belong here.

I want to take her picture, stinky roll-up cigarette and all.

Red stares fondly at the girl like she's her long-lost bestie. Which must be exactly who she is. Apparently I'm about to score a new friend, without even having to try. I feel warm, all over.

"The Pavilion?" the girl says, in case I haven't understood, jabbing her cigarette at the big peach-painted block on the Pier. "There was a band on. Think they're playing all summer. I can't wait for next weekend, they were wicked lush."

Red leans over my shoulder. "This," she whispers, "is where you say, *Oh, that's my parents' band*, and the phenomenon known as 'conversation' ensues."

I open my mouth.

I clear my throat.

No words come out. None at all. Not even stupid ones.

The girl lifts her sunglasses and looks me up and down, with a tiny frown.

"Now would be good," whispers Red, with a touch of urgency. "Oh come on, Blue! This is Fozzie! Your future best friend, Fozzie! This is where it starts. Talk to her! Just open your mouth and—"

Her hands grab my shoulders, to push me to talk. But Red can't grab me. Her hands sink into me, slow, eerie. A wave of cold and damp washes over me head to toe and I feel queasy, the horizon tilting as if we're on a boat, the whole world tipping upside-down and cold cold cold—

And then I throw up all over the girl's purple boots.

4. THE SHED

I don't know what's worse: the fact that I puked on my future best friend's boots before even talking to her, or my mum having to come and collect me. With a plastic bag of spare clothes, just in case, as if this is playgroup and I've had a trouser accident.

"I can't believe it's you!" says Fozzie, when she finds out that the mum she called from my mobile and the pregnant drum-smashing ninja from Joanie and the Whales are one and the same. "I was just going on about how much I loved the band when she got poorly."

"People loving on your parents: enough to make anyone vom," says Mum, handing me a bottle of icy water. "How're you doing, Bluebell? Any more to come up?"

I wish people wouldn't talk about sick when you feel sick. I can still taste chunks, even though Red's not around to set me off again. By the time I'd stopped hurling, she'd vanished.

I shake my head gently. "I am so so sorry about your boots," I croak at Fozzie.

"We'll get you new ones," says Mum. "Pay for them to
be cleaned, maybe?"

"Don't you dare," says Fozzie. "It's not the first time
they've ended up in a bucket. Punters throw up on me all
the time. Well, they do when there are any."

She jerks her head towards the silent Red Dragon roller
coaster, outside. We're in the fairground, in a little café
called The Shed. Apparently Fozzie's parents own it, along
with a couple of the other stalls in the fair, so she works
here all summer as a waitress.

She has a job. Like a grown-up.

The Shed sells orange tea in plastic cups, and whippy
ice cream. Stale popcorn swings in pointy plastic bags from
the serving hatch. Every few minutes, the wooden walls
shudder, and glass jars of sugar walk across the tables as the
Whirler Twirler next door gets up to top speed. Not that
anyone's riding on it. The fairground's practically empty.
All the rides are up and running again, except for the Red
Dragon – but the POLICE INCIDENT sign and the
strings of blue and white tape across the gates aren't much
of an advert.

"Electrical fault, that's what I heard," Mum says.

"Yeah, that's what they reckon," Fozzie sighs. "It
happens sometimes, even in the big theme parks. All the
safety stuff kicked in, exactly like it's supposed to. If that
little kid hadn't tried to climb out, she'd have been right as
rain. Should never have been let on in the first place, mind
you. That's our fault, that is: management negligence.
Tommo, who was running the ride? Lazy beggar wasn't

41

checking the line carefully enough. He's been given the boot, of course, but, not exactly good advertising, is it? And, well, if she'd have fallen. . ."

Fozzie blows her cheeks out, whistling softly.

I lay my forehead on the cool sticky table. Breathe in. Breathe out.

My mobile buzzes, vibrating through my skull. A text. From Red.

Does this work? it says. I ignore it. That is a waste of 10p right there. I don't know what to text back, anyway. *Hi. Sorry I vomited all over your best friend's shoes?*

Punters throw up on me all the time, Fozzie said. I'm a punter, not her friend. Just another tourist.

"Summertime Blues" by Eddie Cochran starts to play from the crackly speakers over the counter. Fozzie starts to sing along in a surprisingly low, gravelly voice as she sashays round the tables, wiping them down. Mum tells her they're planning to add it to the set-list, and Fozzie's eyes light up. She and Mum break into muso chat, about the band opening the Fifties Fest later in the summer, and where Fozzie's heart-shaped sunglasses came from.

Great. Now she's going to be best friends with my mum instead.

There ain't no cure for the summertime blues. . .

I stare out at the empty funfair as it starts to rain. Pirate ship, its flag flapping damply. The famous faces painted on the backdrop of the Whirler Twirler, only halfway familiar: Lady Gaga's second cousin, Beyoncé's evil twin. A little wooden booth painted to look like a gypsy caravan, with a light bulb in a crystal ball perched on its roof, not quite straight. MADAME SOSO, FAMOUS CLAIRVOYANT, it says outside. Inside is a grumpy-looking woman in a skew-whiff purple wig, eating a hot dog. She's got ketchup on her chin, and no customers. You'd think someone who can see into the future would be able to avoid that sort of thing.

"Stick around, if you like, Bluebell. It's going to be dead all day. I'll be stuck talking to myself otherwise," says Fozzie.

Mum gives me an encouraging look, and I feel a tingle of hope.

"Might get busy over lunchtime. But I've got a little sister," Fozzie goes on, pointing at a small girl outside. She's leaning against Madame Soso's, watching the Frogger Flipper where you can win a misshapen fluffy dolphin, three goes a pound. She looks about eleven; twelve at most.

That's what Fozzie really means. Take your flowery shoes and go and play at the kiddie table, little girl.

My mobile buzzes again.

OMG! IT DOES WORK! EVEN THOUGH IM TXTNG SAME NUMBER!

"Looks like you're in demand already, mind," says Fozzie, nodding at my phone as it buzzes a third time.

There's a rattle at the serving window by the counter, louder than the Whirler Twirler, and Fozzie slides it open.

It's the two guys she was with last night: the chubby pirate and Top Hat Boy.

"All right, Fozz," says the pirate, though he's not actually dressed like a pirate today. "What's all this I hear about some tourist yacking on your feet?"

Top Hat Boy lounges against the window, looking bored. Fozzie laughs with the pirate – a big hoot of a laugh, like the seagulls outside, *argh argh argh*. She lights another cigarette, muttering an explanation and jerking her thumb my way.

Even Top Hat Boy almost smiles.

"Can we go? Please?" I whisper to Mum, my face crimson, and pull her to her feet.

"Bye then, thanks, sorry about the sick," Mum calls over her shoulder, waving the plastic bag as I drag her away, leaving behind the friends I'll never make.

I'm going back to bed. Preferably for a year, until all this is over and I'm someone else.

Dad makes me a soft-boiled egg with toasty soldiers, like when I was tiny, and brings it in to me on a tray. I sit up in my bunk bed, the top of my head pressing against the ceiling, Milly tucked under one arm.

This is what I really want. Not to be thirteen. To be a tiny nuggety peanutty baby kept safe by my mummy and daddy, for ever.

Halfway down my egg, the back of my neck prickles. There's a sudden draught, like a window being opened.

"Hey," says Red, brightly. She's standing in the one empty spot of floor, between a tower of Jane Austens and an abandoned pair of jeans, unzipped, still half-holding the shape of Tiger's body like a second skin. They'd make a good photograph, but I don't reach for the camera. I don't want Red thinking I want a picture of her.

"Feeling better, then?" she says, eyeing my plate hungrily.

I pick up a strip of toast and dunk it firmly into the warm egg, a trickle of yellow goop escaping over the lip of the shell. Crunch crunch crunch. Then I lick my buttery fingers, one, two, three.

Red looks like a puppy. A kicked one. I want to punish her, but being mean is hard.

"Go on, you can have some toast, if you want," I say, grudgingly.

She gives me a weak smile. "Can't," she says, jabbing her finger at the plate. It slides right through the toast, dissolving into smoke, then re-forming itself, like it did before. "Apparently I don't need to eat. But it's like when you've just stuffed your face, and someone gives you the dessert menu, and there's a big picture of a chocolate brownie on it. I'm not *hungry*. I'm . . . wanting."

I don't like the sound of *wanting* for a whole summer. Then again, she has just ruined my whole life, so maybe it's fair enough.

I eat another bit of toast.

"You're angry, aren't you?" Red says, ducking her head so her hair flops over her face. "About The Bench, and the, er, upchucking."

"Did you know that would happen?"

"No! Time-travelling wishes don't come with a manual, you know. Nobody told me I was going to go all wispy and not be able to eat toast either. It wasn't exactly fun from my end either. You know that thing when you need to be sick, but you can't actually throw up? Like that. Yuck. I know I'm sort of here to hold your hand through this summer, but, trust me: we are *not* doing that again."

She looks greenish at the memory.

"If you didn't know, I suppose it wasn't exactly your fault," I mumble.

"I swear, I was only trying to help! I knew Fozzie would be there. I was being . . . encouraging."

"When this was your summer, is that how you met Fozzie? Puking on her boots?"

"Er. No."

I push the tray away with a sigh. "So that's it, then. It's all gone wrong already. Fozzie's not going to be my friend."

Amazing, grown-up Fozzie, with her job, and her roll-ups, and her heart-shaped sunglasses.

"Of course she is!" Red makes to punch me on the arm, then snatches her hands back, holding out her palms in apology. "Look, it's like this," she says, hopping up on to the other end of the bunk; looking relieved, even surprised, that she doesn't wisp right through it. "Um. OK, imagine the future is a map, right? There's a road on the map called Bluebell Jones, with planned-out predictable points on it, like . . . bus stops. Big unavoidable events, like your birthday." She grins. "And in between are all these little things on that road that don't matter so much; stuff I did when it was my summer. Reading a book. Eating a boiled egg. So: Bluebell Road is there on the map, already planned out, right? But if you've got the map, you can see which things are bus stops, and which ones are boiled eggs. You can climb on a motorbike and take a short cut, get to where you want to go a bit quicker. Maybe jump a fence. Skip a few miles of road completely."

An odd look flits across Red's face; as if she hadn't realized that was something she knew.

I like the sound of Bluebell Road. Speeding towards my Red future, even quicker than first time around.

"Hang on. You said I was supposed to ignore maps." I frown. "Throw away the itineraries and the timetables and maps, you said."

She's perfectly still but for her eyes, darting, curious, looking somewhere else. Then she blinks as if she's only just heard me. "Yeah! Only – not this one," she says, shaking her head with a smile. "This one's special."

"*You're* the map?"

"I've seen the map. And I guess I'm another stop along the road, too. And I'm the motorbike. OK, it's a terrible analogy. But you get the idea."

I do. Sort of. "Me throwing up on Fozzie: was that on the map?"

She hesitates, looking uncertain, then grins again. "That was a wrong turn," she says proudly. "A detour. The right road's still waiting for you. We just need to get you back on to it. Trust me, Blue."

It's dusk when we take the short-cut path down the hill together. The fairground lights glitter, beckoning. My cat's eyes, marking out the road.

It's Sunday night, on the first weekend of the summer, but the crowds are still staying away. The other rides are back up and running, pumping out tunes and sirens. *Get your tokens at the kiosk*, says an American voice, optimistically. *Remember to ride safely!*

"Want to go on that one!" squeals a whiny girl, pointing at the Rock'n'Roller, spewing out the chorus of "We Will Rock You" over and over. Its single row of seats are empty but for one. But the Red Dragon's still caged beside it: lights out, striped tape flapping in the wind. The whiny kid is dragged off, with promises of a pound in change for the slots in the Lucky Penny. She's not the only one.

"Party dress, no one to dance with," murmurs Red, eyes glinting as she watches the Wacky Gold Mine's empty carts bounce along the tracks.

I don't like Penkerry, or fairgrounds, but even I feel sad.

At The Shed, it's no different. No real customers. Just the pirate (back in costume, this time) and Top Hat Boy, the little sister, and Fozzie, leaning on the counter, yawning, heart-shaped sunnies still perched on her nose as she chews gum.

We linger outside, in the shadows. I do, anyway. Red beams, marching for the door till she realizes I'm not following.

"Come on, this is perfect, the gang's all here!" she says.

"The gang," I whisper. "I was going to have a gang."

48

"You still will, you berk." Red wraps her hands tightly around her bare arms, gleefully jigging on the spot. "I haven't seen them in so long! That's Dan: he's the pirate. He's not really a pirate, obviously. He works at the Doughnut Hut by the pirate ship. He's hilarious. And that's Mags, Fozzie's kid sister; she comes off quiet, but she's pretty smart."

Red laughs, as if she's remembering something from her own summer, from the road. She looks so happy. I hug my arms, too.

"And Mr Top Hat?"

"That would be Merlin," she says steadily, looking up at the sky.

"*Merlin?*"

Red rolls her eyes. "Yeah, *Bluebell*, want to make something of it?"

God, I hope they don't call the little one Milk-Thistle.

"Oh, hello," says Red, as a door slams. "This could be interesting."

It's Madame Soso, the fortune teller. She's locked up her booth, and is now stamping her way into The Shed. Fozzie stops leaning at once. I can see why. Soso's a solid lady. Quite the vision, in her purple wig, sleeves billowing, the bells on her shiny floor-length skirt tinkling with annoyance.

We follow her, and slip into the first booth by the doors, unseen.

"All right, it's like this," announces Madame Soso, in a brutal accent. "I've had no custom all bloody day. I know Tommo got the sack for letting that kid ride without checking, but the punters don't care about that. All they see is those police barriers, and no one's lifting a finger to get them shifted."

"That's not fair," says Fozzie, folding her arms defensively. "Mum and the other traders are meeting with the insurance investigators every day. They're doing everything they can do."

"I don't care, love. If trade doesn't pick up by tomorrow, you can tell your mam from me, she can keep her booth. I'll be out of here."

Red grins, and starts to whisper instructions, urgently, in my ear.

"And don't go thinking you can just pick up a clairvoyant of my calibre," Madame Soso continues. "We talk, love. On the spiritual plane."

"What happened to no fun without surprises?" I whisper. "Isn't this cheating?"

(No one notices me talking to thin air. They're all staring at Madame Soso, holding her fingertips to her head and crossing her eyes when she says "spiritual plane".)

"Yeah, it's totally cheating," Red whispers back cheerfully. "That's the difference between you and me, Blue. You like rules. I like breaking them."

She jerks her head, frantic, till I clear my throat.

"Excuse me," I say.

They all turn to stare at me, and for a horrible moment I am only Bluebell Jones: strictly backstage, no audience involved. She doesn't steal scenes. She ruins them by being tongue-tied and pathetic.

But not tonight. I've got Red, feeding me my lines.

"Madame Soso, isn't it?" I repeat after Red, all politeness. "Sorry to interrupt, but I couldn't help overhearing. You really should stick around. That accident was local news; no one's even going to remember it by next weekend. The Red Dragon will be open again next week, on Friday. After that Penkerry will be as busy as ever."

Madame Soso sneers. "And how could you know possibly know that?"

I catch Red's eye, her graceful wing of hair. "I can see into the future," I say, all innocence. "Can't you?"

Dan and Mags both snort. Madame Soso's head snaps around, and they fall silent. When I let my eyes slide over, I can see them both shovelling fistfuls of chips into their mouths, Dan's shoulders still shaking with silent laughter.

"Hello. It's Dan, isn't it?" I say.

Dan's shoulders go still.

"And Mags. And. . ." I narrow my eyes, as if listening, then produce a dreamy smile. "*Merlin*. Of course. It's very nice to meet you."

The three of them stare at me, amazed.

"Honestly, Janet, I'd stay right where you are," I say, turning back to Madame Soso. "You don't mind me using your real name, do you? It is Janet? Mrs Janet Butcher, from Port Talbot?"

Madame Soso juts out her chin. "Soso is my professional name."

Fozzie coughs, placing a perfect, polite smile on her face. "That's settled then. I'll tell my mum you want to give

51

up your booth," she says, "though there's a penalty clause in your contract, for leaving without notice. You'll forfeit your deposit, lose your percentage of the gate money for the whole month. But it looks like we'll be able to replace you without any trouble at all."

Fozzie smiles pointedly at me.

Madame Soso gives me a glare.

"No thank you," she says, hotly, then wafts an arm over her face, unfocusing. "The mists of time are parting, and my spirit guides happen to agree with this amateur you've got here." Her eyes return to piggy focus. "Tell your mam I'll be staying on, all right?"

She gives her purple wig a fierce tug, like a tip of a hat, then whirls and stomps back to her booth, jingling.

I let out a breath I didn't realize I'd been holding, as Red gives me a round of applause.

"Oh my god, that was brilliant!" says Fozzie, sliding out from behind the counter. "How did you do that? I swear, I didn't tell her your names. Guys, this is – Bluebell, right?"

"Blue," I say. "Just Blue."

It's cute. Like a nickname.

"Let me shake you by the hand, you bloody gorgeous thing, you!" says Dan, grabbing my hand in both of his. "Loving your work. About time Soso got a kick up her clairvoyant backside. I'm Dan, but you apparently know that, you freak."

"Yep. And you work at the Doughnut Hut, by the pirate ship."

"Nah, I just happen to like dressing up like a pirate: it's

52

total coincidence," Dan says, "unlike the size of my gut, which comes from eating the merchandise. That's because our doughnuts are irresistible – and special offer for today only, my lovely, it's three for a pound, made fresh for you by my own fair hands, tossed in golden sugar before your very eyes. Best food in the fair, bar none."

"Oi!" yells Fozzie, marching over to take back what's left of his plate of chips. "Second best, you meant?"

"Course," he says, looking pleading till she slides the plate back. "Sorry. It's hard to turn the patter off – and I've not had much chance to use it today. The doughnuts are tasty, though. Serious."

Mags pokes him in the squishy bit of his tummy, Dan wraps his arm around her throat in a fake strangle while she fake-pummels him, and I realize, earlier, Fozzie never meant to send me off to the kiddie table. Her little sister is part of the gang, a mate like the others.

"Nice to meet you, Mags," I say, smiling extra hard. Mags shrinks her shoulders, smiling shyly.

Top Hat Boy slides out of the booth. "Merlin the Magician," he drawls, his accent a little softer than Dan's, hazel eyes circled with smudgy eyeliner. He flips his hat off to reveal dyed-black hair, falling into his eyes; the hat tumbles down one arm, to land perfectly in his hand. "Always enchanting to meet a fellow illusionist."

He delicately bows, takes my hand, and presses his lips lightly against my fingers.

I yelp and snatch my hand away. "Sorry!" I squeak, regretting it instantly. "I – didn't mind! Only I was a bit surprised. People where I come from don't do things like that."

"People round here don't do things like that either," says Mags wearily.

Dan claps an arm around Merlin's shoulders. "Merlin here is what we call a *special* child. That's why we gave him the hat: so you can see him coming and run away."

Merlin rolls his eyes at me, as if to apologize for the company he keeps, and flips the top hat expertly back on to his head with a flick of his wrist.

My hand begins to twist behind my back, unbidden, trying to copy the movement. I want to know how to do that.

Maybe he'll teach me. Red'll know.

I look round, and spot her perched on the counter, legs swinging in their boots, an odd proud smile on her face.

Thank you, I want to say. Red nods her head minutely, like she hears it anyway.

Fozzie pushes me on the shoulder to sit in the booth, squeezing in beside me. "So come on then, you little star: spill," she says, bright red lips curving. "How did you do that? With the names?"

I can feel Merlin's scrutiny, those hazel eyes trying to see through mine. The others think it's funny. He really, truly wants to know.

I look over at Red, swinging her feet.

I flash them a grin, and tap the side of my nose three times: tap-tap-tap.

54

5. THE FAIRGROUND CRAWL

Mum covers Peanut's ears whenever Dad swears, her hands pressed on either side of her bump, and when he rolls his eyes she says, "Don't mess with Team Peanut: we're buddies, we're an 'us'. Where I go, it goes."

He apologizes to her tummy and calls her "we". *Would we like a cup of tea? Will we be taking up all of the sofa, or is there room for one more?*

I'm half of Team Red, now. She's not my baby (obviously: urgh). She's better. My constant companion. We giggle together on the trip to the chocolate factory, as she moans enviously at the free samples. When my handwritten itinerary has scheduled Penkerry Attraction Number 6: Cliff-top Crazy Golf, she puts new words in my mouth – *I'm going to the fair instead, OK?* – and I play pinball with Mags, drink coffee (black, sugary) with Fozzie while she smokes and Dan eats chips. At night, Red reads my book over my shoulder, and tells me not to sleep yet because there's a good bit coming up.

She sits on the sink and watches the family eat dinner, like we're her TV.

It makes me feel special.

On Friday, as predicted by my remarkable clairvoyant self, the Red Dragon reopens.

I'm in The Shed, showing Fozzie my camera. She thinks the chunky buttons are "tidy", and wants one for herself.

"Go on, take her picture," prompts Red, watching us with her feet up on a table – so I do: unicorn Fozzie, an empty ice-cream cone held to her head.

"More horns!" Red shouts, pointing fingers like a bull on her head, and I shout, "More horns!" too, till Fozzie makes like a Viking. Then she tucks them inside her shirt, giant pointy norks thrust proudly forward – at the exact moment an older couple walk into The Shed to buy takeaway teas. I hide behind the camera, embarrassed, as Fozzie laughs her seagull laugh, and serves them anyway, shirt stretched tight, and Red nearly falls off her chair laughing.

Red's so funny. I didn't know I was funny.

I love us three, hanging out together.

We're interrupted by an amplified roar, the stink of petrol, and as I peer through the Shed doors, the huge fanged head swings into life, eyes blazing.

The POLICE INCIDENT signs are gone, along with

the stripy tape. The Red Dragon, empty of riders, rattles effortlessly around the tracks. A huge plume of flame shoots into the sky.

"Oh my god," breathes Fozzie, throwing the cones away and hurrying to the door. "They did it! Mum said they were going to beg the insurers to sign it all off by this weekend, but I never thought. . ."

"The beast is alive!" yells Dan, throwing off his pirate hat as he sprints towards me, Mags and Merlin following behind. "Let's crawl!"

A fairground crawl. Fozzie explains it, as she gleefully flips the "closed" sign on The Shed and pushes me outside. Every single ride, in a row: no stops, no get-outs.

"No throwing up," says Dan with a wink at me.

No chance. I'm not getting on any of those things. I catch Red's eye as she watches me anxiously, then turns away, fiddling with something.

My phone buzzes in my pocket.

Pretend I'm calling you so we can talk?

I blink, then mime surprise, and vaguely jab at the screen.

"Um. Hello?" I say awkwardly, holding the phone to my ear. "This is Blue. Which, um, you would know, because you called me, so. Um. Who is this?"

"Wow, I am never letting you improvise again," says Red. "Now shut up and listen. I know what you're thinking. *I don't do fairground rides, they're scary and they go fast and sometimes they get stuck upside-down and people nearly fall out of them, waah waah waah.*"

"I don't sound like that."

"You do inside your head, when you know you're being a whiny little crybaby."

I glare at her – then tone it down when I realize Fozzie is behind Red, and thinks my glare is for her. I plaster on a quick smile.

"Look," I hiss, spinning away from the group. "I can't do it. You know I can't."

"What if I know you can?"

I blink.

"Trust me, Blue. This is on your road. You never know: you might even enjoy it."

I look at her: smiley-faced T-shirt, chunky boots, flaming red hair dangling over one eye. She's a pushy pain in the arse, but she's still who I want to be.

If she can do this, that means one day I'll be able to. So I might as well start now.

We buy baby-blue wristbands from the kiosk, the ones that let you ride all day.

We start small: Dodgems, and Teacups; the slow gilded horses of the old-fashioned Carousel.

Merlin gets his long spider legs stuck inside the red London bus on the Funtown Merry-Go-Round. We go off to do the Whirler Twirler. When we come back he's still there, knees tucked up around his ears, mournfully going round and round. We're all laughing so hard I can barely take his picture.

Haunted House. Pirate Ship. A nasty one called the Domino Dancer, which leaves Dan green and sweaty because he "doesn't do sideways".

We hesitate outside Madame Soso's, but she glowers at me from under today's wig (red, with silver streaks), and slams the booth shut.

Wacky Gold Mine, Rock'n'Roller. We ride them all.

Last up, the Red Dragon.

Madame Soso's gloom about the fairground's future was rubbish. There's a crowd around the number one ride again already, a queue at the gate oohing every time the plume of flame leaps into the air, licking at the tail of the dragon but never catching it. Whenever it makes its stop in the centre of the biggest loop, the whole fairground seems to hold its breath – I can see the girl, her hair hanging down, her shoulders slipping out, that breathless moment before she was caught – but the flames spurt up, the cars glide through the rest of the loop, again and again. Safe. Not dangerous. Perfectly, legally approved, police-checked, safe.

I can do this, I think, all the way to the front of the line. *I did the others, I can do this one.*

But the dragon's yellow eyes blaze at me, and suddenly I can't move. There's an empty seat next to Mags, in the last carriage, by the tail. They're all beckoning me on board, but I shake my head, backpedalling through the line. I don't care what Red says about road maps. Nothing is going to get me to ride that thing.

They clang the gate shut. Smoke begins to billow from the dragon's mouth, and they're off, without me. With Red instead. I see her hair blowing in the seat beside Mags: hear her yells of delight as they rattle round the curves, through the corkscrew and up to the big loop.

I can't look and can't look away, both at once.

They hang upside-down. Red lets her arms hang too, waving.

The plume of flames shoots into the air, snapping at their dangling fingers – but the cars are already moving again, bringing them safely back to earth.

I'm trembling, shaky, wondering what they'll say. What she'll say. Stupid Blue, scaredy-cat, whiny little crybaby.

But everyone else is trembling and shaky too, and no one says a word about me; not the gang, not Red. We tumble together laughing at the snapshot they show at the end: the four of them at the exact moment the flames go up, mouths open, eyes like eggs, Merlin with both hands clamped over his top hat and a look of sweet possessive panic on his face.

Red gazes at it too beside me, windswept and glowing, her eyes bright.

She's not in the picture, but it doesn't matter. I know she was there.

That night, Joanie and the Whales play the Pavilion again.

I wish them luck from backstage, again, then skid along the boards of the pier and back to the dark dance floor, pushing through the crowd. I'm not going to dance tonight, like last week – but this time I don't mind. I'm

Blue. I'm here to take pictures. Dancing's a few more miles down my road.

I weave through the people until I find Fozzie, all dressed up: bright red prom dress, lippy to match, and she's wearing her purple boots again, though they stink of disinfectant. Beside her Dan's got tissues stuffed in his nose, like crumply white moustaches. Mags is at home – no gigs for her, too young, and I'm guiltily pleased that's not me. No Merlin, either. ("Who knows where Mr Mystical goes off to," Dan said, when I asked, sharing an eye roll with Fozzie.) I feel a pang of disappointment, though I don't know why. It's not as if he says much.

Tiger's sitting on the bar with the elf girl and a crowd of friends, drinking the free tap water.

I mess around with the camera buttons, the chunky clip-on flash, wishing I knew what I was doing, squinting through the viewfinder. I still miss the digital screen. Till I print this first film, I won't have a clue whether any of these pictures will come out at all. It's photography Red-style, I guess. No fun without surprises. I'm safe with this subject, anyway: Tiger can make a blurry, badly lit smartphone snap look like art. Her eyes always seem bigger and bluer in pictures, her neck long, swanlike. Not quite human. Sometimes I wonder how she can really be my sister; if Mum and Dad found her on the doorstep, hatching out of an egg.

I snap one shot off, at the precise moment the lights drop, the precise moment her smile widens.

There's a hush.

Dad steps out into his spotlight as Mum settles herself behind the drum kit, and I realize the Pavilion is packed. Maybe it's because it's later in the summer. Maybe it's Tiger and her magnetic tendencies, drawing them in like the tide – but it's as if people aren't passing by or there by mistake, like most of the Whales gigs I've been to over the years. Dad's going to get a big head. I can see him glancing back at Mum, and they both look white and wowed.

I spot Red at last, perched on a speaker stack at the edge of the stage, hair blazing crimson at the edges where the spotlights hit, gazing down on the band.

Dad straps his show-time face on. "It's good to see you here, Penkerry," he drawls in his best Vegas voice. "Now show me what you got."

They rip into "Johnny B Goode", and the glitter ball drips light across the surge of bodies.

The bass thrums up through the floor, loud enough to pound in my chest. My chair shakes. I hold Diana out, up, and snap the bob of the crowd, the band onstage. Too far and too fast for focus, so they'll be blur and light.

Tiger dances with the elf girl, as if there's no one else on the dance floor.

Dad stuffs up the lyrics of "Hey Baby", and nearly falls off the stage laughing.

They play "Summertime Blues", and Fozzie launches into gleeful, uncoordinated arm-flailing, too adorable to critique. Dan plays air guitar and tries, briefly, to scoop Fozzie into a proper rock'n'roll dance hold, which goes sideways when she tries to dip him. He's so surprised he ends up doing a slide between her legs, and they both fall over, lying flat and floppy with laughter.

It's their best gig ever. They play three encores, and the last one even has people listening to it.

I meet them backstage like always, to help them get the gear up to the car.

"Top night!" yells Fozzie, as Dad locks up the backstage door. "See you around, Blue!"

I wave back as she dances wonkily along the pier.

"*Blue*, now, is it?" says Dad, smirking. "I see. I think we need to reassess our naming strategy for Peanut, honey. Stuff flowers, let's go with colours. Vermilion? Or Aquamarine? Orange?"

"Heliotrope!" shouts Tiger.

"Beige," says Mum. "My granny always said you can't go wrong with beige."

"Beige Jones: future rock god," says Dad thoughtfully. "If you say so, sweetness."

We get to the car, parked up on the prom, and Mum and Dad have a snog while we pile things in the boot. They're always like that when the gig goes well.

Tiger wolf-whistles. I give them a slow clap.

"Thank you, thank you, we're here all summer," Mum says.

"Well, I think you can say we're officially settled in," says Dad, as we pile in and drive off. "So, my gorgeous girls: what do we think of Penkerry?"

Tiger's smile is electric. "Love it," she breathes.

Dad quirks an eyebrow at me in the rear-view mirror.

"It's good, yeah. It's, um. . ." I look at the lights from the pier, reflections flickering on the black water as we head up Penkerry Hill, hunting for the right word. "It's . . . *tidy*."

"Ha!" yelps Dad.

"Oh my god," says Mum. "You've made my children Welsh."

"It's in the genes, sweetheart!"

"I know this dents your patriotic pride, love, but you were born in Kent."

"Ah, but I grew up here, that's what counts. Welsh parents. Welsh grandaddy. It all counts."

We pick out Welsh names for Peanut all the way up the hill, to add to the list on the fridge. I hope we call Peanut "Myfanwy". That way, if we're going to buy her Myfanwy-themed birthday presents, we'll have to come back.

"Hey, can we come to Penkerry next year? For my fourteenth birthday?" I ask as we climb out of the car. I'm so happy. There's nowhere else I'd want to be blowing out my birthday candles – but Red had to wish herself back here from my next birthday. Maybe I can fix things so we come back for real. Like an advance present, from my old self to the new one.

"Sure, baby," says Mum, waddling up the caravan steps. "Why wouldn't we want to come back?"

Red's waiting inside, and I beam, proud of myself.

Red looks at the carpet.

She doesn't say a word.

6. THE BOY WHO DOESN'T LIKE TO BE TRICKED

"What do you mean, you've got plans?"

Dad steals the Marmite out from under Tiger's hand and holds it hostage.

Tiger fights him for the Marmite with a teaspoon.

"I'm going out. With Catrin. She does t'ai chi up in this place in town, and I said I'd go and check it out with her. You *know* I've always wanted to learn t'ai chi."

"Of course you have," says Mum, even though Tiger's never mentioned t'ai chi before in her life, as she plucks the teaspoon and the Marmite out of their hands and clasps them in front of her. "So, this Catrin: she's who you've been out running with, in the mornings?"

Tiger nods, toast in mouth, humming.

"Think I might have seen her around," Mum says, casually. "At the Pavilion, maybe. Short dark hair? Lots of silver jewellery? Gorgeous?"

Tiger hesitates, toast hovering. "Suppose she is a bit," she says. "She's just a friend," she adds quickly, the words *at the moment* trailing in the air behind.

"Mmm. Well, bring your 'just a friend' round for tea sometime, will you?" Mum says, smiling as she slides the Marmite back across the table.

Tiger rolls her eyes, but I can tell she's pleased. Tiger's potential girlfriends are not always parentally approved. Or sisterly approved either, not that anyone asks me. We all hated Sasha the Cow long before she broke Tiger's heart and turned her into a weeping snotmonkey.

"She could come out with us today," says Dad, flipping through the diary I brought with us: the handwritten itinerary we've been cheerfully ignoring. "What haven't we done yet, Bluebe—" He coughs, correcting himself. "Blue? Ah, here we go: boat trip out to Mulvey Island. I used to love it over there. Proper sandy beach. Come on, my bucket and spade's getting rusty."

"Um. Actually. . ." I mumble, shrinking my shoulders. "I'm doing that already. Going on a boat trip to Mulvey Island. Today. If I'm allowed? I checked – they have life jackets. And the boats come back every hour till seven, so I wouldn't be late. I'll take my phone."

I look at Mum as a smile spreads across her face. "Well, aren't you organized? Sounds fab, baby."

I don't know why I was so worried. It was Red who came up with the idea: of course they were going to say yes.

"You going with Fozzie?"

"Yep. And her sister, and a few other people. I'm supposed to bring a fiver and something for lunch."

"Never mind about that," says Dad. "I'll come with you. It'll be like a daddy and friends day out. I'll bring my guitar!"

"Dad!" says Tiger.

"What?" he says.

"Ignore him, he's joking," sighs Mum.

"Am I?" says Dad.

"Um," I say, "it's a public boat, anyone can get on it . . . so I suppose. . ."

Mum takes Dad's hand. "Ian, love: remember that night we brought a tiny little Tigerlily home from the hospital, and then a few years later we had Bluebell, and we both realized we'd never have any time to ourselves, ever again, until they were grown up enough to do their own thing? Well, now they are. This is when our glorious new era of freedom starts." She gives her rounded belly a pat. "And it's going to last less than three months before it goes away again for a very long time, so shut the hell up. OK?"

"Fine," sighs Dad. "A day with my lovely wife it is. What do you want to do, my darling?"

She yawns. "I want you to do the washing-up and then be really quiet while I go back to bed."

She kisses him on the cheek and shuffles off.

"Rock'n'roll lifestyle, romance, glamour: I am living the dream, ladies," says Dad, pulling on rubber gloves with a snap.

I leave him to it, hugging Mum's words to myself like

they're my new Milly. *Grown up enough to do their own thing.*

Cash in my pocket and sarnie in my bag with Diana, I hop down the caravan steps, and nearly walk straight into – or through – Red.

"Why are you out here?" I whisper, hurrying away from the caravan in case my voice reaches through the walls. "You can walk right in, remember?"

Red shakes her head. "Feels rude. And weird. And, I don't know, there could be naked people in there! You should be happy I don't just barge in unannounced."

I suppose I am. I haven't got any bits and pieces that she's never seen before, but still. It would be like taking off all your clothes and staring at yourself in a mirror. I skipped that PSHE homework. It's freaky enough looking at my body walking around as Red, and she's got pants on and everything.

"So, all set for the boat trip, huh?" Red says, looking me up and down. "Got your swimsuit?"

"Yep," I say, lifting up my T-shirt to tug at my swimming costume, on under my clothes.

Red looks surprised. Almost as if she knows I nearly didn't put it on; nearly left it scrunched on my bunk, oops, by mistake, how silly of me to forget my humiliating Lycra one-piece, the one that shows off the puppy-fat belly where there should be a waist, the flumpy parts where there should be boobs; hairy bits, spotty legs. . .

Of course she knows.

"Is that what you did?" I ask her. "Left it behind?"

She blinks at me from under her hair. "Doesn't matter," she snaps. "Can we just go?"

On the way down the short-cut path, I want to ask her whether the boat ride will make me feel sick – but Red's quiet. Quiet, or cross. Maybe I wasn't supposed to wear the swimsuit after all. When this was her summer, she didn't have a Red poking her nose in to remind her. She probably did leave it behind.

But then, she knows that – so if she didn't want me to change what she did, why did she even ask? My brain hurts even trying to figure it all out. It's like I'm watching the most complicated episode of *Doctor Who* ever, starring me. Twice. And I don't know how it ends.

Instead, I think about photos I want to get today – the lighthouse, the view back towards Penkerry, the improbably blue sky – and begin to feel excited again. I've got twelve shots left on this roll of film, and another roll in my bag just in case, though I'd rather get the first set developed first: see what I'm getting right and wrong.

The Mulvey Island boat bobs at the end of a floating wooden jetty that juts out from the beach, at the far end of the prom. By the time we get there, Fozzie and Mags are on board, waving. Dan's there too, joking away with the boatman like an old mate.

The jetty shifts under my feet as the water moves it, and I instinctively reach to grab Red's arm for support before I remember, and shoot her a relieved grin. She doesn't grin back.

"Where's Merlin?" I say, hanging back.

I look up at the handful of houses clinging to the cliff at this end of the beach; pick out the grand-looking white one Fozzie told me was where he lived.

"He's always late, miserable beggar," shouts Dan over the slapping sound of the water against the boat. "Come on, Blue, don't be shy!"

I expect Red to climb on board first – but she's walking back along the jetty.

"Hey!" I shout. "Wait, stop!"

"Is it Merlin?" says Mags.

"Can't see him," says Fozzie, craning her neck.

"It's all right, love, we're not leaving for a minute or two yet," says the boatman.

Red keeps on walking, on to the pebbly beach and up. I open my mouth to shout again, but they're all looking at me like I'm barmy already. Thankfully Merlin appears at the head of the promenade, top hat bobbing, tailcoat flapping as he runs.

"You've got good eyes," says Dan. "Come on, you lazy git!" he yells.

Red's still walking away. I whip out my phone, mutter something incomprehensible about having forgotten to do something, and call her.

Red stops, halfway up the beach, and answers just as Merlin flies past.

"Where are you going?" I hiss, cupping my hand round the phone.

Red turns round, her shoulders tilted like she's tired.

"I'm going to leave you to it for today," she says.

"What? No, you're supposed to come with me! You have to come with me!"

"Go and enjoy yourself. You don't need me. You're going to have a brilliant time, I promise."

She hangs up, and I watch her walk slowly up the beach, head down as the wind whips her hair. I don't understand. What could Red possibly have to do? She can't touch anything. She can't talk to anyone who isn't me. And anyway, she's *my* wish person. She's here to help me, not go off and do her own thing.

Doesn't she want to spend the day with me?

"Everything all right?" asks Fozzie, as I clamber awkwardly on board. "If you want to invite another friend along, go ahead. We don't bite."

I crunch up my face, trying to work out what part of the conversation she might have overheard. I'm not sure, so I just shake my head and smile.

"Forget it, doesn't matter."

Fozzie nods and sits back, though I can feel her eyes on me, curious, as Merlin hops on board just in time.

The engine rattles into life, and we go puttering off through the water, leaving Red far behind.

The first few minutes are fine, but as we get out into open water the boat stops gliding through the water and starts bouncing off it, jolting from side to side. I wish Red was here to promise me I'm not going to fall in, or throw up. Unless that's why she didn't come: because I am. Fozzie's wearing flip-flops and even she might not forgive me puking on her bare feet.

"That's the Bee," says Mags, pointing out a stack of rock jutting up from the sea near Penkerry Point, which the boat chugs around at a careful distance. It's black and shiny, with three fat stripes of some kind of yellowy-white rock running through it. "Means we're more than halfway there," she whispers, shifting over to sit next to me. She spends the whole of the rest of the trip talking softly in my ear, asking me to show her how Diana works; distracting me on purpose.

I tell her about my wall of pictures in my bedroom at home; my tessellating pattern, personal wallpaper.

"You should do that in your room," says Mags, nudging Fozzie. "Her bedroom is rank," she smirks.

"It is," sighs Fozzie. "That bumpy wallpaper with the little bits of wood stuck in it, painted pink. Euch. I got a few posters, but I never thought of using photos. That would look lush."

"You can have some of these," I say, holding the viewfinder to my eye.

"Really?"

I click: pin her bright red smile in a blue sky, for ever.

The water's calmer once we're nearer Mulvey Island, and by the time we reach the jetty there, I'm feeling almost normal. There's no beach on this side: a landing platform, and a steep path up the rocks. We scramble up and out on to the flat, where the wind's so strong it sends Mags skittering along, almost lifted off her feet. Merlin carries his hat, hugging it close to his chest. My jumper billows out in front of me, and I rest my hand there for a second, trying to imagine a Peanut inside. Mum says it's like being a microwave oven, buzzing away with a light on inside – but no convenient ping to tell you when it's done.

We pass the lighthouse: automated, so it's all locked up. I take a few shots that will have strings of my hair whipping across the frame.

When we dip down into a hollow, the wind drops at once, and a golden beach with frothy little waves sparkling in the sun spreads out below us.

"Aieeeeeeeeeeeeeeeeeeeeeeee!" yells Dan, as he begins to sprint down the path, shedding clothes as he runs.

I half expect Fozzie to be too cool for seawater; not with her hair sculpted, and her face so perfectly made up. But she yells, "Come on," eagerly chasing after him, Mags on her heels. They fling bags down by a patch of rock at the top of the beach, then strip off, swimsuits on under their shorts like me, and follow his footprints through the wet sand to splash into the sea. I can hear Fozzie yelping at how cold it is, and Mags runs straight back out again, knees jumping high. Then she laughs and runs back in, splashing Dan with a vengeance.

If Red was here, I guess she'd be hissing in my ear, urging me to follow them.

I should. It's only a body. I'll have a new one soon, one like Red's. Who cares if they see the not-quite-finished version I've got now?

Merlin flops down next to the bags, leans back against

the rocks, and plonks his top hat back on to his head, half over his face like he's going to sleep.

"You're not going in?" I ask.

He tilts the hat up. "I don't swim," he says, and drops the hat brim back over his eyes. Then he lifts it again. "I *can* swim. I just, you know. Don't."

He crosses his ankles, slides his hands inside their opposite sleeves as if they're cold, and yawns.

I look at the splashy happy people in the water.

"I don't swim either," I say. I drop my bag down. I stretch out beside him, and it's that simple.

It's not quite that simple.

This is the first time it's been the two of us, alone. I don't know Merlin. I know he lives in a big white house. I know he doesn't have an official fairground job, but whenever we pass a deckchair, he plucks playing cards from his pocket and launches smoothly into his patter, Find The Lady, Pick A Card, all gentleman's charm and hand-kisses for the old ladies in return for a quid or two. I know when he switches it off, he sinks out of sight. He looks like he's been drawn into technicolour Penkerry by a different artist, with pen and black ink: a little black cloud in the blue sky.

I just don't know why.

He answers my questions – yes, his accent's a little different from the others', he was a proper Valleys boy till they moved when he was ten; no, he doesn't have brothers or sisters; yes, I can try on his hat – but it's all shrugs and mumbles, like he's at the dentist and I've got the drill.

It's only when I shut up and take out my camera that he relaxes. I click away, shifting near to the water to capture Dan's wide mouth, Fozzie's legs up in the air as she handstands underwater. Then a few close-ups: Merlin's battered Converse frosted with damp sand. The crinkled red rose tucked into his hatband. The angle of his nose against the blue sky, cheekbones and chin shadowed by the hat brim, bottom lip dangling plump and unaware.

It's a good face. For photographs, I mean. I stare at it through the viewfinder. Not taking any pictures. Just looking.

He shifts when he realizes, wrapping his sleeves tighter over his chest, though I can feel my arms itchily pinking in the heat from the sun.

His cheekbones are pink too, in two high spots.

I lower the camera, suddenly understanding. "Sorry. I hate having my picture taken too," I say.

He frowns at me from under his hat, like I've stolen something he didn't know he had. "Suppose that's why you're the girl behind the camera," he says dryly.

I fiddle with the lens, wondering if it's that obvious to everyone else.

Merlin idly watches the waves for a moment. Then he seems to make a decision. He sits up, tilting the hat back so I can see his eyes, smiling charmingly behind their rings of eyeliner. He reaches into his coat pocket for a deck of cards, shuffling them deftly with his long thin fingers, eyeing me like a dare.

He doesn't see me as a friend, then. Only a mark, one of the tourists he tricks on the prom.

I nod towards the cards as they flick together. "So what do those make you?" I say.

"I'm the boy who doesn't like to be tricked." He's smiling, assembling all his charm, but I don't think he's joking. "Confession time. The Red Dragon reopening on the Friday? Lucky guess, fine. But how did you do the rest of that riff on Madame Soso? Fozzie swears blind she never told you those names."

Merlin keeps his eyes on the cards as he asks, but I realize he's serious; genuinely desperate to know.

"I told you," I shrug. "I can see into the future."

He stares at me intently, as if hoping the eyeliner will hypnotize it out of me, then drops his head with a low chuckle.

"You're good," he says. "It's almost like you believe it. Go on, then." He slides the deck out in a fan on a flat bit of rock. "Which card am I going to pick?"

"Oh, I'd need my, er, spirit guide for that. And she's not here today."

"Really?" he says, witheringly. "What a shame."

"You think? I'm kind of enjoying the peace and quiet."

It's out of my mouth before I've even thought it. But it's true, I realize. It's a relief, not to be concentrating on not talking back to someone no one else can see. Not trying to live up to her expectations.

"Cheers, says a lot for my company," Merlin says ruefully.

"Oh, I didn't mean—" I blush. "I only meant. . . It's nice to just be yourself, sometimes, you know? Instead of trying to be something you're not."

His eyes travel over my face. I don't know what he's looking for.

We play Guess the Card on the flat bit of rock, and he gets it right every time.

I wait for him to switch back into charm mode, dip his hat for me to throw him a coin, but instead he hands me the cards, and starts trying to teach me the trick. I play at reading his mind: *Two of clubs. Three of clubs? A club? A diamond? A card of some kind, with maybe a number on it?*

It makes him laugh out loud.

Lunch is a messy picnic, everything we've brought piled on to a sandy towel, help yourself. My sandwich and banana look feeble. Fozzie and Mags have Shed goodies in packets. Dan's brought cold pizza and doughnuts and a bottle of Coke. Merlin's is all shop-bought fancy stuff, Mexican wraps and posh crisps – and I wish Red was here after all for me to yell at her, because foodfail is exactly the kind of thing she should be rescuing me from.

No one seems to mind, though. Everything tastes like sand and suncream anyway. Dan eats the banana, under protest at the idea of unprocessed food entering the sacred temple of his body, and we give him a round of applause.

Fozzie scoops all the rubbish into a plastic bag, and we take it to the bin together.

"Hey. Thanks for hanging out with Merlin," she says, once we're too far off for them to hear. "He always says he wants to come, and then he just sits there looking like a sad crow, and we all feel crap about having a laugh without him, even if it's his own fault."

"Oh. That's OK. I don't mind."

"You don't have to, though. I know he's a weirdo. He wasn't rude to you or nothing, was he?"

She puts a cigarette between her lips, her hand fumbling with the lighter awkwardly.

"Oh, look at me. That's 'cos I feel bad, 'cos that sounded awful, didn't it? I do like him, don't get me wrong. But, well. You know. All that 'ooh, I'm so spooky and meaningful' stuff's a bit much. And there's the whole nerdy magician thing."

"Is that nerdy? I thought it was cool."

Fozzie brushes sand off her face, wiping at the smudges of washed-away make-up. She nods, and laughs, *argh argh argh*. "Yeah? I suppose it's that, too."

Penkerry's so different. At home, things are either in or out with Grace and Monique. They don't get to be nerdy and cool at the same time. I haven't thought about Grace for ages. I wonder what Bali's like, and realize I don't really care.

We lounge around on towels while lunch goes down, watching kids and dogs mess around as the next boat arrives and the beach gets busier. Dan and Fozzie roll more cigarettes, while Merlin does big fake coughs, and Mags pretends to die of a tragic lung disease. Fozzie blows smoke in her eyes, as revenge.

Fozzie, Dan and Mags go back in the water.

I hesitate. I could strip off, right now, and follow them. I should. It's what Red would be telling me to do.

But I'm not far enough down Bluebell Road yet. We'll come back here, I know it. I'll get another chance. Instead I dig a hole with my hands, letting the light golden stuff trickle through my fingers; scooping the darker, damper sand out and building a mountain, a castle, a mermaid lying marooned on the beach. I spend for ever sculpting her face: smooth cheeks, curved chin. Her nose crumbles as the sand dries out. I try to fix it, but the rest crumbles too, ruined. It's weirdly upsetting.

Merlin says, "Hey," and curls a finger, beckoning.

By the time the others stagger back up the beach, ready to finish off Merlin's posh crisps, I have learned how to flip a top hat on to my head with one sharp flick of my wrist.

Nearly.

"She got it twice in a row earlier, no lie," says Merlin, as attempted demonstration number three bounces off my nose. "All down to the excellent teacher, of course," he adds.

Fozzie catches my eye and gives me a grateful nod.

I manage it on the fourth try: not straight, and it's too big so it slips down over my eyes, but undeniably square on my head. It earns a round of applause, and I skip triumphantly up the beach and on to the steep path off the beach before Merlin can snatch it back off my head.

"Oi! You let that blow away up there, there will be consequences!" he shouts, and I remember to clamp my arms over it just in time, as I reach the top of the slope and get hit by the wind.

I stand up on the top, gazing out across the sparkling water, to the stripy Bee rock, to Penkerry. It looks tiny and unreal from here: a strip of pebble beach, pier, the fair just a flicker of sunlight on metal.

I want a photograph, but I've left the camera on the beach.

When I turn to fetch it, Diana's already in Merlin's hands, already lifted to his eye. He makes the shot before I have time to hide.

"Hey!" I yell.

He lowers the camera and shrugs, exaggerating it so I can see from up here.

"You steal my hat, I steal your camera," he shouts, the words drifting on the wind alongside laughter as Fozzie and Mags team up to tackle him.

He sounds smug, and I run down, to point out to him that I've got the sun right behind me, and even if he's got the focus anywhere close to sharp and the framing anywhere close to me, that shot will never come out. But I stop a few footsteps down, just enough to be out of the tearing wind. This is the picture I want to take. Not Penkerry in miniature, but this, them, today, right now: Merlin half-buried under sand, Mags and Dan trying to drag him into the sea, Fozzie doubled up laughing. Me and my friends, on Mulvey Island.

I suck in breath, sharply. That's why Red didn't come.

This wouldn't have happened if she'd been here. If she were here I'd have been waiting for her to tell me what to do, what to say, how to get it all perfect.

And instead, I've lived it.

My phone rings in my pocket. I'm smiling already as I pick up, ready to tell her I understand; to thank her for showing me I could do it by myself.

"Hi, look, I can't really talk," I whisper.

"You don't have to talk, just listen," says a breathy voice, loud. I stare at the caller ID. It's not my number ringing me. It's Tiger's.

"Are you still on the island? How soon can you get back?"

"What? I mean, why?"

There's a scrumply sound, like someone blowing their nose.

"It's Mum," says Tiger. "She's in the hospital."

7. MUM

It takes thirty minutes for the boat to arrive, another twenty-five to make the crossing, fifteen more in the back of a taxi to the hospital, a damp twenty-pound note from Fozzie clutched in my hand. Too long.

Tiger isn't answering her phone.

Dad neither.

I don't try Mum's.

By the time I find the right room in the maze of plasticky corridors, I've imagined every awful thing that could possibly have happened, twice.

"Oh, baby, look at your face," says Mum, sitting up in bed looking pink and healthy and perfectly well. "Everything's fine!"

Dad's on one side of the bed, reading the newspaper. Tiger's on the other, tying one side of Mum's hair into tiny plaits. They don't look panicked. To be honest, they look pretty bored.

My shoulders drop, and the bowl of fear in my insides

empties out.

"What's going on? I was . . . I thought. . ."

"Come here, darling," says Dad, folding up the paper and standing, beckoning me over to sit in his chair. "What the hell did you say on the phone, Tiger?"

Tiger shrugs. "Mum's in the hospital, come back now. Something like that?"

"Nice," sighs Dad. "Reassuring. Not going to give anyone heart failure, that."

Tiger squints. "Sorry. Didn't think."

"What happened?"

Mum grabs my hand and squeezes it twice, fast like a heartbeat. "Nothing major. We went for a walk up along the cliffs, and I had a bit of a funny turn. Thought for a minute Peanut was going to try to make an early entrance."

Dad rolls up his sleeves. "I was all set to be the heroic father delivering his own child, but your mum crossed her legs and held it in, like a wee."

Can you do that? I think to myself.

Mum slides him a look, and he kisses the top of her head, leaving his hand resting there, stroking.

Probably not.

"Were you frightened?" I ask.

Dad's hand goes still on the top of her head.

Mum squeezes my hand again: one two, one two.

"Only for a second. Only when we didn't know what was going on. I had a little bit of bleeding, which has stopped now, and they've given me some stuff to make sure it won't start again. And I need to take it really, really easy.

But, baby, we're both going to be fine, the doctors say it's all manageable." She smiles. "To be honest, I'm pretty sure half of it was indigestion."

"Extra large chips *and* a White Magnum," whispers Dad.

"Eating for two!"

I decide now is not the moment to quote that article in *Health* magazine about expectant mummies not really needing extra calories. She wasn't impressed last time.

"I'm sorry I wasn't here," I mumble, fiddling with my sock. It's got Mulvey Island sand in it, gritty between my toes.

Mum shakes her head and tells me it's fine, she's fine, there was no need for me to rush back here at all, that she'd much rather I spent my day in the sun instead of fretting in here for no reason – but I'm only half-listening. There's a movement behind me, soft low breathing.

I turn my head and Red's there, leaning against the wall just inside the door.

She's been here all along, taking my place.

"How could you?"

We're in the smelly bit by the bins round the back of the hospital café, where I'm supposed to be fetching cups of tea for everyone. I'm shouting and if anyone passes there are far too many men in white coats standing by to cart me off for talking to myself, but I don't care. I don't think I've ever been this angry before.

Even Red looks shocked. "Calm down, will you?" she says. "Mum's fine. 'Peanut' is going to be fine." She makes air-quotes round the word "Peanut", like she wants to rub in the fact that I still don't know its name, when she does. When she knows *everything*.

"I know that now! But I didn't before. I was terrified! And you *knew* everything was going to be OK!" My heart twists. "You even knew this was going to happen today, didn't you? That's why you wouldn't get on the boat this morning, isn't it?"

She shuffles her shoulders, hands stuffed into her pockets. "That's . . . complicated."

"No it isn't. You did this on purpose. You lied, so I'd go off to Mulvey Island without a clue, and you could stay behind and be with them."

"Yeah. No. It's not what you think." She runs her fingers through her hair, tucking the wing behind her ear. It makes her look so much more like me: blameless Blue, only doing her best.

I get it now, how annoying that is.

"I did want you to go off and do it on your own. That totally was part of it. Did you go swimming? What was it like?"

She sounds bright, as if she expects me to launch into happy sharing time about sunburn and picnics.

"Brilliant, yeah, I was off building a sandcastle while my dad was phoning an ambulance. What a great day, lucky me. Only, if I'd known Mum was going to get ill I'd never have gone. *If only* there was some way I could've peeked into the future and seen it coming."

I've never been this sarcastic before, either. It's like I'm turning into all the narky bits of Red in one go.

"But that's why I didn't tell you! If you'd known, you wouldn't have gone off on the boat, you'd have stayed behind worrying and fretting – about something you couldn't do anything about. Apparently." She swallows, flipping her hair over her eyes again and staring moodily at the floor. "Knowing the future doesn't mean you can change it, Blue. I thought, maybe . . . maybe I could drive us down a different road. But there are fixed points: big, unchangeable moments that even a wish can't take back. Some things are going to happen, whether you want them to or not. Things you're better off not knowing."

"I don't believe that."

"You will," she says softly. She shakes her head, meeting my eye and smiling again. "Short sharp shock, like ripping off a plaster: that's the best way. Not watching and waiting and knowing too much. Look, it was a compromise, OK? I figured since there are two of us, we'd get the best of both worlds. You could go off and hang out, do the whole Mulvey Island thing, and I'd stay back and look after Mum."

"You're invisible! How is that looking after her? She didn't even know you were there."

"Maybe she did," Red shrugs. "She might have, I don't know, *sensed my presence* or something."

"I don't want her to!" I shout, chilled by the thought. "Leave her alone, all right? She's *my* mum."

"She's my mum too," says Red evenly. "Come on, there's

more than enough of her to go round at the moment, right? We can share."

She laughs, as if she can smile her way out of this.

"No, we can't. She's not your mum. You don't need a mum. You're not even a real person. You're just a wish."

She steps back as if I've pushed her, her shoulder melting into a wisp of smoke when it nudges the wall.

"See?"

Her face closes down. "Yeah, that's me: your wish come true," she says bitterly. "You get my help, and all the rest. Friends to hang out with, a shiny new camera, happy happy family time with Mummy. Did you ever stop to think about what I've got out of this deal? I don't sleep. I don't smell, but oh my god I need to have a shower, change clothes, change *anything*. I've watched the beautiful glorious sparkly sunrise over Penkerry Pier every single morning and guess what? Bored now. I've ridden the Red Dragon twenty-seven times in a row: not scary any more. While you've been tucked up in your bunk bed I've sat in the cinema listening to people crunching their way through popcorn I can't eat, while some hot actor guy says the same lines over and over again, and he doesn't even take his shirt off – which I know already because he didn't take it off the first time and it's the same bloody film, over and over and over. You're the only one I can talk to, the only person I could ever tell – only you don't even care."

"I'm supposed to feel bad for you because you're *bored*?" I'm the one laughing now, though nothing is funny today.

Red goes very still. "So that's it? I'm here for you, to

rescue you – and that's it? Doesn't go both ways?"

"What would *you* need to be rescued from?"

Red looks down at the ground, up at the sky, and finally at me. She opens her mouth, words on her lips, but she catches herself, and looks me dead in the eye.

Then she raises one finger, and tap-tap-taps the side of her nose.

Mum gets discharged that afternoon, and Dad drives back to Penkerry at fifteen miles an hour.

We spend the evening with all four-and-a-half of us curled on the narrow caravan sofa, my head tucked neatly on top of Mum's bump, watching bad reality TV and eating blueberries. A superfood, packed with antioxidants.

If Red's outside, being too polite about potential nudity to come in, I don't care.

That night, I dream we are a family made of sand: Dad, Tiger, and a sleepy smooth-cheeked Peanut-baby, held close in Mum's arms as they ride the Red Dragon.

Red's not there.

I'm not there either.

When they reach the top of the highest loop, the ride gets stuck, upside-down. They crumble. They trickle out like sand emptying from a bucket, my golden family disappearing one by one.

8. SILHOUETTE

I like being Head Nurse.

I like our new routine.

Tiger's alarm goes at six thirty every day so she can go running with Catrin, so I'm awake early anyway. When I hear her come back in and run the shower, that's my cue. Breakfast in bed for the poorly lady, freshly squeezed orange juice and toast (no honey, no peanut butter).

Then we transport all the pillows and duvets on to the sofa, and make a nest. Dad's got a new deal going with Deirdre, the Pavilion manager: handyman for the week, to make up for the band having to skip a few gigs (under protest, but none of us is letting Mum touch a drumstick right now, doctor's orders) – so I grab a lift with him down into the town to do the day's shop while Tiger takes over.

I like pushing the trolley by myself. I like having a list. It's mostly leafy things to make soup and the brown kind of pasta, but Mum says if some Coco Pops accidentally fall into the trolley before I get to the checkout, that's just one of those things.

In theory I'm off-duty in the afternoons, but I don't like to go too far. I like being with Mum, just us. We talk about school, and the Fairground Crawl, famous photographers and songs that it is apparently criminal that I don't know.

Mum fusses about me missing my holiday, but Penkerry comes to us instead. Fozzie drops in between Shed shifts, sitting at Mum's feet to hear war stories from all the bands she's ever toured with, and offering traditional Chinese suggestions for the list of Peanut names on the fridge.

"Nothing hard to say," Fozzie warns: she's Xiao Xing at home, Daphne on her school reports. Neither fits like Fozzie.

Peanut should have a Goldilocks sort of name, I think. Not too hot or too cold, not too big or too small: just right.

Catrin brings scented oils and gives Mum a shoulder rub that makes her doze off in seconds.

"I can do your shoulders too, Blue," Catrin offers, wiping lavender oil off her hands.

I glance to Tiger, in case she's eye-rolling, waiting for little sister to leave. I wasn't allowed to even speak to Sasha the Cow (not that she ever spoke to me). But Tiger says, "You should, Blue, she's *so* good," so I tuck myself up on the floor, cross-legged.

"Hmm, knotty here," says Catrin, prodding a hurty bit of my shoulder, the smell of menthol making my eyes water. She massages my forehead, hard. "Lot of tension around your third eye."

I sneak one eye open to share a secret grin with Tiger at the woo-talk – but Tiger's nodding along, dreamily watching her. It's cute.

Catrin teaches me, Tiger and Fozzie yoga poses on the threadbare grass outside: Warrior One, Warrior Two, Salute the Sun. Dad comes home to find us all in Downward Dog, saying hello with our bums in the air.

He joins in, obviously.

I run inside for Diana. He's the very last shot on the roll.

Red's always there.

I see flashes of softly blowing crimson hair at the corner of my eye, outside the caravan windows.

I hear her footsteps behind us on our slow pace around the park, on the short-cut path from the beach, tailing me round the supermarket.

It's like she's in the Penkerry wind. In every pebble on the beach. Everywhere.

I want to know her secret. What's in our future that made her wish herself back here?

Why doesn't she want to go back?

But if I stop to ask, she'll know how much I still need her.

I drop my first ever Diana film in to be developed, and two days later, it's done. Time to launch Operation: Cover Up Fozzie's Nasty Pink Walls.

It's like stepping into a temple to fifties teenage dreams. Fozzie's bedroom is so *her*. The walls are icky pink, true, and the carpet too. But her duvet cover is a pattern of flamingoes on a sky-blue background, and her dressing table is stacked with rollers and pins, cherry clips and liquid liner. The shelves are crammed with DVDs and importantly thick books on films. Surveying it all is a single poster, black and white, of a guy in a white T-shirt and jeans, lounging against a classic car.

"Say hi to my boyfriend Jimmy," says Fozzie huskily, flinging herself on to the bed and blowing the poster a kiss. She's wearing short jeans and a polka-dot shirt, hair scooped up in a red scarf and her smile a slash of cherry-red.

"Wow," I mumble, perching, feeling very young and too clean. "I thought that was a real picture – you know, like a real old one. . ."

Fozzie crinkles her face as she lifts up her head. "Blue, that's James Dean. *James Dean?* The most famous movie star of the 1950s? Or . . . ever?"

"Um. He looks a bit familiar?"

I shrink my shoulders, half-expecting her to send me home in disgust, but Fozzie gasps, thrilled.

"Oh baby, have we got some stuff to watch." She hops up and starts tugging DVDs off the shelf, shaking her head. "I cannot believe you're going to get to see *Rebel Without*

A Cause for the very first time. Jealous! And *Giant*. Hey, have you ever seen *Streetcar*? Oh my god: mini Liz Taylor festival, right here, right now. Love it!"

She hesitates, eyes bright, balancing two DVDs in her hands like she's weighing them.

"Which first? What do you think?"

I toe the floor with the rubbery edge of my flowery shoe.

"*Choose*," she urges, thrusting both at me. "I've seen them a billion times, I don't care."

I shrug, worried suddenly that I'll pick the wrong one – but that isn't the right answer either.

"Oh, right, you're not fussed, is it?" She tosses the DVDs on the floor and climbs on to the window sill, tugging a half-smoked cigarette from a pocket. "Fine," she says, hanging out of the window to light it, a sharp edge in her voice that says it isn't at all. "I mean, I'm just trying to show you stuff I care about, but, whatever. It's my thing, not your thing. I get it."

I blink down at my flowery shoes. They're definitely not "her thing". They're not my thing either. They're me not having a clue what "my thing" is.

Fozzie's the one who knows exactly who she is, smoking out of her bedroom window, surrounded by movie stars and pink flamingoes. All her stuff reflects her back so perfectly, and I gaze round, longing to be that complete, that put-together.

It's not seamless, though. She's got a desk like mine, tucked under the window: pencil case, highlighter pens, neat pile of colour-coded holiday homework. There's deodorant on the window sill (roll-on, extra-strength, 72-hour protection). Peeking from under her pillow are the grubby limbs of a teddy bear, hugged bald.

"Sorry, Fozz. I'd *love* you to show me that stuff," I tell her, and mean it. "But maybe we could do the photos first?"

I pull the envelope from my bag.

Fozzie pops her mouth open wide.

"What am I like?" she says, chucking the end of her cigarette out of the window, all sharpness gone. "You didn't even open them yet. Come on, let's have a look. Open, open!"

Part of me is desperate to peek outside and check that she hasn't set fire to anything (because discarded cigarettes are the *most* common cause of accidental fires, and possibly me and Fozzie ought to have a serious talk about her smoking anyway) – but Fozzie hops down from the window sill, clapping her hands, and she's so excited I don't want to spoil it.

It's like my birthday all over again as I slide my finger under the plastic seam. The paper envelope of prints slides out into my hand, waiting to spill the last two weeks.

Fozzie fans the prints out across the tumbling flamingoes of her duvet.

They're getting out of order.

Her fingers are on the print surface, leaving smudgy marks.

Red doesn't even need to be here for me to hear her voice: *lighten up, Blue, who cares about a few fingerprints?*

But I forget all that anyway once I see the pictures.

"Whoa," breathes Fozzie, as if we've discovered a new colour.

Mulvey Island beach: spray and sparkle off the water as Fozzie leaps, arms up like wings. Mags, squinting at the camera, sitting on a pair of sand-buried legs. Tiger, pale like a marble statue as she gazes adoringly at Catrin, just out of frame. Merlin, sulking on a London bus. Joanie and the Whales, underlit and hazy, before a pulsing crowd. Mum holding one drumstick to point at her Peanut-belly, like an arrow. Dad's bum.

Me, in silhouette, a black shadow perfectly framed by the bright white light of the sun.

It's the picture Merlin took on the island. Low angle so my legs are a mile long, crisp edges on the tufty grass, a blurry halo round the shape of my body, a corona round the top hat on my head, focus melting under the contrast. The chance composition is textbook. I could wait my whole life to take a picture that good.

"That one, wow, you look *amazing*," says Fozzie, staring at the print.

I do. It's the first time I really start to believe it. This odd Blue skin of mine will shape itself into my bright Red future: will contain all of her.

But all I can think when I look at the photo is that in my silhouetted pocket is a phone that will ring, and across the water Mum is already in hospital.

I turn away, hugging my ankles, chin on one knee.

"What's up? Blue – are you OK?" Fozzie settles on her

knees next to me, then her hand goes to her mouth. "Is it your mum? Was it worse than they thought?"

I shake my head. "She's fine. I'm fine, it's . . . it's no big deal. I've just got some stuff going on."

Fozzie wrinkles her forehead. "I could help, maybe? If you told me about it?"

I look at her, neatly folded on the floor, all concern.

I want to. I want to tell her everything, right now. The whole lot.

"I've got this friend," I start. My mouth feels dry, my neck damp and sweaty, and I wonder for a second if there's another one of those vomit-inducing wish rules, like the no-touching one, about keeping Red a secret. "And, well, this person is taking up a lot of space in my brain. It's all I can think about at the moment."

"Anyone I know?" says Fozzie, a fraction too casually, as if she knows what I'm going to say.

"No," I say firmly. "You definitely, absolutely have not met this person."

"Uh-huh," says Fozzie. A knowing smile spreads across her face.

Could she know? Has she seen Red all along? Is that why she didn't mind about the sick on her shoes? Should I really, really tell her, right now?

"This friend of mine, she's kind of doing my head in."

"Oh," says Fozzie, sitting back in surprise. "You said *she*?"

"Yeah."

Fozzie giggles. "Sorry. I thought you were talking about Merlin."

96

"*Merlin?* Why would I be talking about Merlin?" I like Merlin. Merlin doesn't try to mess with my head and steal my mum. Well, he tries to mess with my head a little bit, but only when he's doing a card trick.

"No reason," says Fozzie, blinking a lot. "So, this friend, who I don't know?"

"I really like her, don't get me wrong. She's quite, uh, similar to me. A more *advanced* version of me. What I might be like if I was, say, for example, a year older. Right?"

"Right," says Fozzie, frowning.

"And most of the time, that's all great – and she helps me out – and I'm totally grateful because she is kind of *amazing* and of course I want to be more like her—"

"M-hmm," says Fozzie, still frowning.

"But I found out she lied to me. About something big."

"I never!" squeaks Fozzie.

I blink at her, confused.

"Oh," she breathes, rocking back on her heels. "You don't mean me. It's that girl who phones you up, isn't it? Your invisible friend, Dan calls her. Only joking. God, check out my big head. Sorry."

She looks mortified.

"I wish it was you I was talking about," I say into my knees. "You make a lot more sense."

"Bloody hell, she must be trouble. So what did she lie about?"

I shake my head. "It's complicated."

"You're worse than Merlin!" she smirks. "OK, so what are you going to do? She a friend worth keeping hold of?"

"I don't know," I say, knotting my hands. "Don't know if I even know her all that well."

"Does she have a good reason for doing what she did, for lying to you? I mean, from her point of view?"

"That's not the point. Her point of view doesn't matter."

"Does to her," Fozzie says, looking at me sideways. "Not being funny, but if you think that, doesn't sound like you're very good mates in the first place."

I can hear what she's not saying. *I'm* not a very good mate.

I wish I could explain why I'm not being a horrible person; not when Red is the lucky one, perfect and seamless and already ready to speed off into my future.

"Invite her round here," Fozzie suggests. "Go on! I'll get Dan to bring doughnuts. They fix everything. Or are you ashamed of us?"

She leans in and elbows me jokily, stale smoke on her breath, a forced edge to her *argh argh* laugh.

"Thanks. I might. I'll see. Forget I said anything, yeah? Come on, let's cover up some of this pink."

Fozzie looks at me sideways a few times, suspicious, maybe disappointed – but once we start piecing the prints together, she's all smiles again.

Mags taps on the door, and coos when she sees the prints.

"You're an amazing photographer," she tells me, shyly picking up a shot of her on the beach, on Dan's shoulders. The colours pop: blues and greenish-yellows, brighter than life.

"It's all down to the camera, really," I mumble, but I glow all the same.

Mags joins in. We decide to frame James Dean, matching colours or clashing them, filling up gaps and spaces with overlaps before starting to tack them to the wall.

"I can't take all of these," Fozzie says, sliding me some of the Mulvey Island beach shots. "You *have* to keep that one for yourself," she adds, passing me the top-hat silhouette.

"And I don't know what that was meant to be, but you can have that one too," Mags giggles, tossing me a bland-looking sea view.

It's Penkerry Point, on a murky day. Nothing special, grass and grey sea and some cloud.

Something special: the first photo, the one I tried to take of Red, the morning after my birthday. Red was right. It's as if she was never there.

I pick up the top-hat silhouette shot and hold them side by side. Red, invisible. Me, a black shape against the sun, empty space.

Two photographs of me, and I'm not in either of them.

It's like the photograph of Mum, drumstick to her belly: a picture of Peanut, though there is no Peanut yet. Part of the family. My family. Not there, and always there.

I hate Peanut.

I've never admitted that before. I don't think I even realized it till I thought it out loud in my head.

I hate Peanut for coming along and changing everything.

I love it, too, love it madly. But there's a corner of my heart – an alveolus; maybe two – that hates.

I hate Red too, just a little.

It aches, knowing I'll never be good enough by myself.

My brain ticks backwards. I look at Fozzie's purple boots, askew in a corner; stare at the top-hat photo and wonder if I'd ever have got on that boat to Mulvey Island without Red's help. Something tugs at the back of my mind; as if I'm looking directly at something, and it's so obvious I can't see it.

I remember what Red said outside the hospital, about watching the same movie over and over, knowing all the words. That's what this summer is for her. Action replay. No surprises.

No wonder she's lonely. I'm the only friend she's got in the world right now, and I've shut her out.

I bite my lip, and listen to the seagulls wheeling outside, *argh-argh-argh*.

I watch *Giant* on Fozzie's mum's sofa without seeing it, and text Red on the way home.

Sorry.

She texts back: *Me too.*

I reply: *No me.*

She texts back: *No you*, and then, a minute later, *Yes, I am wasting 10p from the future. Suck it up.*

That night, I pin the top-hat silhouette and the empty

patch of grass to the ceiling above my bunk bed. My secret selves, watching over me while I sleep. When we go home, I'm going to rearrange my room. Paint, maybe, a few posters, to reflect my Redness back at me.

I sneak into Mum's handbag and pin up the fuzzed black-and-white printout of Peanut's scan too, to say sorry for that unkind corner of my heart.

In my dream, Peanut has a mobile phone, and texts me daily.

Grew 6 millimetres today.

Body now covered in fur, like a monkey.

Tell Mum not to have curry again, it makes me uncomfy.

I text back questions: *What's it like in there? Are you warm enough? Is it dark?*

Peanut's ringtone is one of those long loud ones, and it makes Mum wriggle, though only we know why.

9. THE CAVE

"So what do I wear?"

It's a Wednesday afternoon, Dad's on nursing duty, and tonight I've been invited to something called "The Cave".

"How should I know? What do you want to wear?" Red's lying on my bunk bed, gazing up at my pictures.

"At least tell me if it's going to rain or not?"

She rolls over and peers out of the narrow window. "Looks a bit cloudy," she says.

I give her a stare.

"What am I, a weathergirl? I don't know. A summer's a long time to keep track of. I don't remember eating four Weetabix for breakfast this morning either," she says, with a meaningful nod at my overfull tummy.

"I had a light lunch," I snap back, sucking in anyway.

And I'm going to be you next year, I think: you, with your boobs and your waist, so I can eat what I like.

I pull out two different tops and hold them up for

comparison, like they do on TV makeover shows. I'm not sure what I'm supposed to be looking for. Mainly I'm just checking for tomato ketchup blobs. "Look, if you won't tell me the weather at least help me out with the fashion. Which one looks older?"

She gives me a hard stare. "Which one do *you* like, Blue?"

I glare back. Opinions are fine for hipster people: the ones who fell in a vat and developed an acute case of Topshop. Me, I'm fashion-blind.

"I wished you here to help with exactly this kind of thing," I growl.

"Yeah. Your wish came true and time-travel was invented so I could help you pick an outfit."

I glare at her, decide on the spotty one at random, and turn my back, self-consciously pulling up my top to change.

"You're ridiculous, but no, I'm not looking," sighs Red as I peek over my shoulder, her eyes locked on the ceiling. "This photo's amazing, by the way. Who is it in the picture? The sunshine silhouette?"

"It's me, you idiot," I mumble, wrestling spotty cotton and armholes.

"That's you? Wearing Merlin's hat?"

Finally I get my head through the right hole, and tug it all straight.

Red's still got her eyes fixed to the ceiling.

"Yeah." I frown. "But you already know—"

There's a clack from the front door behind me, and

with a swish of the curtain Tiger's home, grabbing me from behind in a hug. She doesn't have much choice, since the room's so narrow, but she lingers, squeezing tight, head on my shoulder, getting her perfume up my nose.

"Hello, gorgeous, talking to yourself again?"

"Um. Yes. I'm funny that way," I murmur, glaring meaningfully at Red.

Tiger spins me round on the spot so she can look at me properly, hands on my shoulders.

"That's OK," she says, breathing in deeply, her cheeks very pink. "We like funny people. We *love* funny people."

She opens her blue-egg eyes wide, and giggles.

"Is she all right?" asks Red.

"Are you all right?" I ask.

"I'm better than all right," sighs Tiger, squeezing my shoulders. "I'm lovely. I'm lovable. I'm beloved."

"Ohhhh," says Red. "*Catrin.*"

"Catrin?" I say.

Tiger's smile bursts out wide.

"I said I love you," she whispers, "and she said she loved me back."

"Oh," I say. "That's, um. Nice?"

It is. I am happy. Of course, she said *I love you* to Sasha the Cow, and Juliet, and a beardy bloke called Elliott during her trying-out-boys phase, and they probably said it back too, and every time not long later there was a lot of sobbing and having to have her hair stroked by Mum on the sofa all weekend – but it would be unkind to mention it.

"I know I've said it before, but it's different this time," says Tiger, slipping an arm round my shoulder and sitting us down on the lower bunk, squashed forward over our knees. "Everything's different. Catrin's exactly like me, you know? Only she's herself too. And she lets me be myself. It's like there was a Catrin-shaped hole in me, like a jigsaw puzzle, and it ached and ached with emptiness and now I've found her I'm complete. She's put me back together again."

I'm pretty sure those are song lyrics, not actual feelings, but the look on Tiger's face says she means them anyway. Every time she says Catrin's name her mouth shyly curves up at the edges. I want to take her picture, but she rests her head on my shoulder, and I can feel the glow coming off her pink face, warming me up.

"Just you wait," she says dreamily, chin on my collarbone, her voice thrumming through my skin. "I know it sounds daft now, but it'll happen to you. When it does, it'll be like the whole world was grey before. You're going to love it."

"Right. OK. Thanks. That sounds good," I say, sliding out from under her arm and standing up, ready to exchange eye rolls with Red. But Red's lying flat, arms back and head resting in the pillow of her hands as if she's not even listening, gazing up with a shy curvy smile on her face, just like Tiger's.

Apparently when I'm fourteen, I'm going to get all dribbly and romantic too.

I like that.

"We're going for a picnic, later," says Tiger. "You could come too, if you like. I want you to get to know Catrin better."

I mumble something about having plans tonight.

"Sounds great! What are you going to wear?" She looks me up and down as I smooth my hands down the spotty top, and this time Red is definitely smirking.

Hours later, I'm stumbling down the short-cut path wearing a huge knotty tasselled scarf round my neck, a flappy white shirt, and a pair of Dad's old jeans, belted so they sort of fit. It's the sort of thing Tiger wears all the time, simultaneously effortless and intentional. On me, it looks like I got dressed in a crashed aeroplane in the Sahara desert, in the dark.

At the end of the path, the promenade is now covered in sandwich boards, and posters hooked on lamp posts. *Penkerry's Legendary Fifties Fest!* Band names fill the space underneath. *Kitty Pleasant. Billie Jo and the Jo-Belles. The Vicars of Twiddly.* Way down at the bottom are *Joanie and the Whales*.

They're in the tiniest writing on the poster, but it's still a buzz. The Fest is on Saturday. Dad's already covered the caravan with Post-it notes with song titles on, rearranging them to get the set list just perfect. He might be a rocker onstage, but I got my over-organized brain from somewhere.

I hurry down the steps on to the beach, skidding on pebbles.

Red scowls and trails along behind me, making me nervous.

"So is it a big cave? Will it be cold in there? Are there crabs and things? Should I have brought food? Will other people be there who I don't know? What happens if I need the loo?"

"You know, Blue, just because I happen to be here doesn't mean you have to spew the entirety of your thought processes at me. Thrilling as they are."

"I'm only wondering."

"You're supposed to wonder! That's what life's for. Embracing the new."

"Hello?" I say, lifting the frondy tassels. "I'm embracing the new! And it turns out the new is itchy."

She snorts, skipping lightly ahead of me on the pebbles, hair lifting off her face, arms splayed one higher than the other for balance.

I wish I could take her picture. I've got Diana in my denim bag, but I know she'd vanish out of the shot like smoke.

I've only got a year to wait before someone can pin her down in a print, though. My heart feels big at the idea, and it hits me all over again: she's me, that's me, that's who I'm going to be. Not guessing or hoping, but guaranteed.

"What are you staring at now, you weirdo?" she says, screwing up her face.

It would be good if I was a bit nicer. Maybe I can

have a quiet little talk to myself, in a year's time, about consideration and thoughtfulness.

"Come on," I sigh, hopping across the rocks more quickly. "I think Fozzie's waving at us."

She's there up ahead, a tiny figure at the foot of a cliff. Up above is Penkerry Point; our caravan too, somewhere too far up and back to spot. There's no way down the sheer cliff except along the short cut to the Promenade, then doubling back along the beach, away from the Pier, along the stretch that's only uncovered at low tide. I can see the lighthouse on Mulvey Island off in the distance, and the Bee rock in between, sticking high up out of the water, with its three yellowish stripes.

By the time I'm near enough to see Fozzie's grin, I can smell woodsmoke, and hear an acoustic guitar being strummed.

"You made it!" Fozzie calls, and the guitar strumming stops abruptly.

Dan shouts something, inside the rock. Fozzie makes urgent shooing motions off to the side, and for a sick moment I think: I'm not meant to be here, I wasn't invited, they're all going to leave now I've come.

I sneak a look at Red and her face is greyish, eyes darting unhappily across the pebbles as if she's thinking the same thing – but before I can turn back, Fozzie's got hold of my wrist.

Three steps up the beach and up again over a pocked, seaweedy slope of solid rock, the cliff splits open into a cavern, high and huge. There's a campfire at the mouth of the cave, sheltered by a dip in the rocks. I eye the flames, wary, thinking of dragons. And fire extinguishers. I bet no one here even cares about the fire triangle. But I let Fozzie push me forward, inside, blinking smoke out of my eyes. There's an instant chill once I'm inside the cliff, the woodsmoky smell mixing with mould and damp.

There's whispering, shapes of people moving in the dark.

A flickering. A set of small flames appears, with Mags's glowing face above them.

"One, two three," someone hisses.

The guitar strums again, and suddenly the cave echoes with *Happy Birthday to You*, as the small flames move towards me.

Someone flashes a phone torch across the cave wall right at the back, high up, to show HAPPY BIRTHDAY BLUE! painted unevenly across the rocky wall, in glossy white house paint.

Fozzie grabs me from behind, Dan hugs me from the front, and Mags holds out a lopsided sponge cake, for me to blow out the candles.

I can barely summon up breath. I don't make any wishes this time. I don't need them.

Then there's a cheer, and more hugging, and I whisper, reluctantly, "It's not actually my birthday today."

Mags shrugs. "Yeah, but your mum said your real one was crap. And Dan never turns down an excuse for cake."

"Hey!" he huffs. "Credit where it's due, it was Fozzie's idea."

Fozzie blushes in the firelight. "Mags did the painting," she says, nodding up at the white letters. "Standing on Dan's shoulders. Team effort."

"You did all this for me?" I whisper, tilting my head to the clumps of people I'm beginning to make out as my eyes adjust, sitting on tumbled rocks, gathered round the guitar.

Fozzie looks embarrassed. "Well, not just for you. I mean, there's always a bunch of people down here when the tide's low enough to get in the cave. It's, like, the party place. But I thought we'd sort of turn it into a party for you as well. Is that OK?"

I hug her again, and tell her it's even better.

She drags me around by the arm, introducing me to blurry faces with names I can't keep track of: Cal and Anya and Marco and Pete, Other Pete and Sarah, with a baby on her knee, cheeks round, dimples firelit. I recognize a few from the Pavilion crowd, the ones Tiger dances with. The guitar girl's name is Verushka or Danushka or something between the two; she's very smiley, either way, and asks me to pick a song for her to play next. I ask if she knows "Summertime Blues", and she laughs, all teeth, and starts playing it right away.

Fozzie squeals, like I knew she would, and starts to dance while Dan sings the words, loudly and mostly wrong.

Mags is chopping up cake and handing it round.

I squint into the darkest depths of the cave, where the ceiling slopes down and the floor slopes up, but it's smelly and colder back there, so I drift nearer to the light and the

110

fire, and find what I hadn't even realized I was looking for: a familiar black shape sitting cross-legged near the cave entrance, framed by the flames.

Merlin, and his top hat.

I slot into place beside him, catching sight of Red hovering just outside, beyond the campfire. I give her a tiny wave, and she smiles tightly, leaning against the rock with her arms wrapped round herself.

She's being kind again, I know, just like Mulvey Island. Letting me feel as if I'm doing this for the first time. Not giving away my birthday surprise.

Maybe I won't need to have that talk to myself, about being nicer.

"Evening," says Merlin, cards in his hands, shuffling them together with a whirr. "What's all this about, then?"

He taps the tasselled scarf with the deck.

"Just thought I might be cold," I say, feeling my face grow pink as I tug the scarf off and tuck it out of sight behind me.

Merlin gives me a narrow knowing smile from under his hat.

"Oh, all right, my sister made me wear it," I mutter, not even sure why I'm confessing it. I settle back against the wall – then tip forward again with a yelp, as the wet slimy rock seeps through my shirt.

"Yeah, you probably don't want to do that," says Merlin, pointing a long pale finger up at the cave walls. They're black, slippery with green algae. Even my painted birthday message has green flecks in it. I look round, and realize everyone else is sitting a careful distance from the walls of the cave.

"Right," I sigh, peering over my shoulder at the mulchy green blobs on white. Hopefully Tiger will be too dreamy-eyed over Catrin to notice I've ruined her shirt. "So – this whole cave is underwater sometimes?"

Merlin nods. "You see the Bee, out there? That's how you can tell what the tide's doing. So long as you can see all three stripes, you can get in and out of the cave easy. Two stripes, you'd better be a good swimmer. One stripe, kaput. Note how I am sitting conveniently near the exit, with a clear view of said helpful rock."

He smiles, awkwardly this time, as if he's letting me into a private secret. I'm glad I told him about the scarf, now.

He shuffles the deck again. The campfire spits and pops as someone throws on more wood, and I feel the extra heat, warming me on one side only. Varushka/Danushka plays that song "Wonderwall", and everyone sings along.

I should probably say something, but Merlin's strange. I don't know what it is; it's like I want to be next to him, but when I am, I'm not sure which me to be.

I pull Diana out of my denim bag.

"Don't," he says, hands stilling.

"I wasn't going to take one of you," I say pertly, focusing on the singers at the back of the cave.

"No, that's not—" he says, and I feel his fingertips brush my wrist, as if he wants to grab my arm to stop me.

I lower the camera, my wrist tingling.

"Sorry," he says quickly, pulling his hand back, flicking

at the edge of the cards with his thumbnail. "I just hate that. It's all anyone does round here, walk through the day going click click click, as if life means nothing unless you can show someone else later. It's not real memory. What do they remember, all those tourists? *Here's where I took a photograph; here's where I took a photograph; here's where I took a photograph.*"

His voice is hard and bitter, and I clutch Diana tightly in my hands.

"I do know what you mean," I say, hesitating. I want to agree with him, to make him feel better. "But photographs can be more than memories. They can be art; something beautiful. They can show you the things you didn't see."

I hesitate again, picturing the prints pinned above my bunk bed: the silhouette girl, the empty space where Red should be. Fozzie's blank look at my unfocused snap of a cloudy square of sky and a patch of grass. The mobile phone in silhouette-girl's pocket, waiting to ring.

"And what's in a picture, it's not only one thing. It depends who's looking."

Merlin's hazel eyes, hiding behind their smudgy rings of liner, slide away from the shuffling cards up to mine. He sucks on his bottom lip, visibly thinking. One eyebrow quirks, as if he can see a different me now too.

"Get us, deep philosophers," he says eventually, smiling, embarrassed.

"Oh yeah," I say, nodding. "Intellectual birthday parties: it's the next big thing."

"Right, right. Happy birthday." He laughs. "So, did your *spirit guide* get an invite?"

"Yeah, she's just over there," I say, giving Red at the mouth of the cave another little wave.

"Eating a slice of cake, right?"

"Spirit guides can't eat cake. Their hands go right through it, like smoke. It's a bit gutting for them, actually."

Merlin looks at me and sighs: fond, like a teacher with a silly pupil. He sits up straighter, presses the cards into my hands, and makes me fan them out, the backs facing me. He sucks on his lip again, skims finger and thumb across the tops, and plucks out one card, pressing it to his chest.

"Come on then, let's have it. Now you say, *I shall guess the card you have chosen,*" he prompts.

His eyes glitter in the firelight, full of challenge.

I nod seriously, then let my eyes drift as if I'm tuning in to some other frequency, directly to where Red is leaning against the rock, the flicker of the campfire between us. All she needs to do is come a little closer, lean over his shoulder, and whisper the answer to me.

But Red's not catching my eye. She's looking at Merlin through the smoke, eyes wide and warm; lips, just parted, curving into a giveaway smile. A Tigerlily smile.

Red likes Merlin.

Red *likes* Merlin. The way Tiger *likes* Catrin.

I look at him again. His eyes glow orange from the campfire. His face is all angles, cheekbones and nose: dark shadows, pale curves. I want to touch his cheek. Stroke it. Run my thumb along his jaw, touch his full lips. . .

114

An "Oh," spills out of my mouth.

"Can't you read my mind?" says Merlin, feigning lightness, his eyes still intense.

"Um. Apparently not today," I say breathlessly, and hope to god he can't read mine.

I like Merlin too.

I've never felt it before, so it might just be smoke inhalation or all those Weetabix, but there's definitely something funny going on in my chest.

Is this why they put love hearts on Valentine's Day things? That's where I can feel it: inside my ribs, a fluttering, like a bird in a cage that's trying to get out.

I want to kiss him. My lips feel tight and tingly. Is that what that is?

I look across the fire to find Red's eyes: for confirmation, that I'm reading this right.

Her eyes are already on me, her face schooled, blank. The moment our eyes meet, she ducks out of sight, away from the cave.

I shiver, and Merlin's face falls.

"You all right?" he says, dropping his card as I shiver again.

He strips off his tailcoat to drape it round my shoulders, his hand brushing my bare neck and sending a quiver down my spine.

He likes me back, the quiver says.

The coat is warm from his body, warm and too big. It smells like spearmint gum and woodsmoke.

"Seven of clubs," I murmur as I stumble to my feet. "Sorry, I have to – I'll be right back, I promise."

"What – oh," he laughs, picking the card off the ground where it's fallen, face up. "That's cheating!" he calls after me.

I throw up my hands in apology as I whirl through the smoke, past the crackly fire and up out of the dip on to the beach. It's dusky outside, and I peer into the gloom, gazing down the beach for Red.

She's sitting on a rock at the base of the cliff, not so far away. It's as if she's waiting for me, though she still looks surprised to see me bundled up in Merlin's coat, tails flapping in the wind.

I stride across the pebbles, not even glancing back to see who might be listening.

"You like Merlin," I say: statement, question, whichever.

"I like Merlin," she says.

"So. Right. So – does that mean he's going to be. Um. My boyfriend?"

Red looks at her hands, tucks her flapping hair behind her ear, and swallows.

"I don't know," she says. "When this was my Penkerry summer, we never even met."

10. A TWO-FLAVOURS PROBLEM

I don't understand. Perhaps some rocks have fallen on my head. Perhaps the campfire has made me sleepy and this is some kind of barmy dream – because Red is still talking in a low, colourless voice, and none of it makes sense.

"Fozzie was never my best friend," Red says, looking at her bare knees. "I never hung around with the fairground gang, not when I was here. Believe me, I wanted to. I was lonely, bored. But I saw that girl nearly fall from the Red Dragon, just like you did: didn't dare even set foot in the fairground for that first week. Even once I had, all I did was watch them. I used to go to The Shed nearly every day; listen to them mucking about, wishing I knew how to start up a conversation. Watching Merlin. Fozzie was always friendly enough, but I was never anything more than a customer. That funny girl who sits in the corner, not talking."

I can't imagine Red being that girl.

But I can imagine Blue doing it. I'd be doing it too, if it wasn't for her.

"Not exactly the best summer ever," Red says. She tries to crack a smile, but her eyes are stuck on sad.

"But you said. . ." I start, but I barely know where to begin. "You said that's why you wished yourself back: because being in Penkerry was so brilliant."

"I lied."

The sea crashes behind me. Seagulls whirl overhead. I can still hear the strumming of Verushka/Danushka's guitar, as if life is going on quite normally, quite naturally, not crumbling at all.

"Don't look so appalled, Blue. People lie to themselves all the time."

"That's not the same."

"I know," she says, looking at her knees again. "I know. I am sorry. But why would I tell you? I got a second chance, one I didn't expect. No sense wasting it. Besides," she says, ruffling her hair back over one eye, "you're a bright girl. To be honest, I didn't think it'd take you this long to figure it out."

"So this is *my* fault?"

"No! But you do get the better end of this deal. You're doing way better than me at living the perfect teenage summer. You've made a bunch of friends, you went out to Mulvey Island, you're hanging out with a bunch of random scene kids at some beach campfire. And don't go imagining

118

I haven't noticed whose coat you're wearing. Me, I just stared at him from afar like a weirdo. You, you're practically flirting."

She smiles, like her old self, all flashy eyes and cheek.

"And you didn't do any of those things," I say, bleakly.

"Rub it in, why don't you? No, I didn't. But you have! So, you know, woohoo. Go Team Blue."

She waves one fist feebly in the air.

"You don't get it, do you?" I say. And she thinks I'm the slow one.

"I've been doing what you tell me to do, all this time," I say, trying to control the wobble in my voice, "because there was a road. Bluebell Road, all planned out."

"There is!" she says. "I didn't lie about that. I told you: some things are fixed, some things neither of us can change—"

"But you're not one of them, are you?"

She looks at her boots.

"I thought at the end of the road was my fourteenth birthday, when I was going to wake and be you. For definite. No mistakes, no chance of messing up. Cast-iron guarantee: no matter how much of a hopeless idiot I am right now, no matter how many detours or side roads I go down, I'm doing what you did. So one day, in the not-too-distant future, I will be you."

"I didn't mean for you to think that," she murmurs.

"And instead? I've been doing the exact opposite of what you did."

"And having fun doing it," she protests.

I shake my head. "But still doing it differently. So I won't be you. Ever. Will I?"

Her face pales, and I can see the flicker: the moment where she wonders if she can lie about this too; the twist of her mouth when she accepts she can't.

"No," she says. "No, you'll never be me."

I nod, my eyes filling up with tears till I can't even see her, and I wonder how your own self can hurt you that much.

She sits on her rock, saying nothing. There's nothing to say.

"Hey, there you are!"

It's Dan's voice, yelling from the mouth of the cave, half hidden by pebbles. He's wearing Tiger's tasselled scarf as a turban, and shouting something about dancing, but then he cuts himself off and disappears. A moment later, Fozzie comes scrambling up out of the dip, looking anxious.

I glare at Red as I swipe the tears away, fumbling in my pocket for a tissue to blow my nose.

"All right? Hey, what's up, what's happened?"

I sniff, chin up, straightening my shoulders out. "It's that other friend of mine," I say, looking straight at Red. "She's let me down. Again."

"And on your fake extra birthday and all? You poor thing," says Fozzie, rubbing my arm. "I did ask around, try and invite her, but your mum didn't know who it was — and you've never told me her name. Sod her anyway. Come back inside and hang with us, yeah? I saved you a bit of cake. And Merlin's all worried, bless him."

Merlin. Beautiful Merlin, who was never on Bluebell Road at all.

"I would." I squeeze Fozzie's hand, trying to smile. "I'd love to. But. . ."

Red's head lifts, and she might not be able to see into my future after all, but she knows I'm saying this to her.

"I need to be on my own."

And I head off back along the skiddy pebbles, past the turn-off to the short-cut path, to walk the long way home.

"Since when is Ben and Jerry's on the official recommended healthy eating list?" Dad complains, dumping the shopping on the kitchenette table. "That doctor's going to string me up tomorrow."

"Tomorrow?" I say, lifting my head off Peanut's bump.

"Just a check-up at the hospital, baby, nothing to worry about," Mum says, smoothing my hair off my forehead with a smile. "And the ice cream isn't for me – though I will have some. Just to keep Blue company."

"Ohhh," says Dad, looking at us curled on the sofa with every pillow and duvet in the van, and Milly tucked under my arm. "Medical emergency. Three spoons coming up."

We perch the carton of Cookie Dough on my knee and dig in. I'm a giant human cliché, but it does make me feel better, just like Mum said it would. We all go for the same big extra-chocolate-chippy nugget at the same time, spoon-fighting. I end up laughing, and I'm so surprised I start crying again instead.

Mum and Dad very politely go on eating ice cream, and don't say a word about my sniffing.

"So," Dad says eventually. "Nice coat."

I shrink into the collar. "I didn't mean to borrow it. I'll give it back tomorrow."

"Sure. So, you'll be giving it back to a boy . . . friend?"

"I haven't got a boyfriend. He's a boy, who's a friend. I think."

I want more than that. My nose is full of woodsmoke and spearmint gum, and the feel of his fingers on my wrist, his hand on my neck. I shut my eyes and see his: hazel, ringed with daring black. My birdlike heart flaps in my chest.

He likes me back. Does he? He does. Does he? He does.

"Right. So the lack of boyfriend, is that why. . .?" says Mum, wagging a melty spoonful of ice cream.

I shake my head, the birdlike feeling fading away. "Argument with a friend-friend. Well . . . a sort-of friend."

"Oh, one of *those*," says Mum.

"Thank god I bought a tub of Chocolate Fudge Brownie while I was at it," says Dad, nodding seriously. "A sort-of friend: that's a two-flavours kind of problem."

"What did the sort-of friend do?" asks Mum.

"Um." I suck on my cold spoon.

It hurts to think about it.

She took away my future.

She dangled the idea of growing up to be exactly who I wanted, right under my nose. Then she snatched it away again.

"One of those 'too complicated for the parentals to follow' type of things?" says Mum, gently nudging me with her elbow so I'll know she's joking at herself, not at me.

Does he like *me*? Or the girl I thought I'd become?

"Complicated doesn't begin to cover it."

"Well, we're here to listen if you want," says Dad, "or we can just be annoyingly cheerful at you. Speak of the devil. . ." he adds, as Tiger comes home.

Tiger springs through the door, flinging a half-empty canvas bag on to the kitchenette table.

"Hello!" she says, loud and bright. "Ooh, ice-cream party, brilliant!"

She grabs a spoon from the drawer and plonks herself down next to Dad.

"And how was your evening?" asks Mum, as if the answer isn't obvious.

"Perfect," she says, sighing. "We put down a blanket and ate sandwiches with the crusts cut off, in triangles, and strawberries. She gave me an Indian head massage. Then we lay on our backs to look at the clouds, and talked about French films and postmodernism."

"Yeah? That's what we do every Wednesday, isn't it, love?" says Mum, slapping Dad's thigh and almost hiding her smirk.

Maybe that's what I'll start doing, now. Merlin and I could lie side by side in the cave, and talk about photography not being evil. He could properly teach me how to flip his hat. I could feed him strawberries.

My brain is so embarrassing. I don't even know if Merlin

likes strawberries. Or me. I don't know anything about him, really. I wonder if I'll ever find out. Red didn't.

"Nice coat," Tiger says, poking at my collar.

"Bluebell borrowed it from a boy, who is a friend," says Dad. "Which isn't at all the same as a boyfriend."

"Really?" says Tiger, flaring her blue eyes. Then she frowns. "Where's my scarf?"

"Um," I say. The last time I saw it, Dan had it wrapped round his head. It could be anywhere by now. I probably shouldn't mention that to Tiger – along with the big green algae stain on the back of her white shirt.

"That's my favourite scarf," says Tiger, her picnicky glee dimming. "If anything's happened to my favourite scarf. . ."

I scoop up a big mouthful of vanilla. I can't deal with a Tiger drama right now.

"You'll get it back, I promise," I mumble, mouth full. "Tomorrow."

She narrows her eyes, then nods, once, and skips off to our bedroom.

"Grabbing a shower," she calls over her shoulder.

We polish off the rest of the Cookie Dough, listening to the speckle of water and Tiger's off-key happy singing: *be-bop-a-lula, she's my baby, be-bop-a-lula, I don't mean maybe.*

My eyes prickle with tears again, and Mum tugs me into a hug.

"Don't stress, baby. If it's worth fixing, you'll find a way."

Dad finds an old Cluedo board in the cupboard under

the sofa, and sets it up on the kitchenette table.

Tiger, dripping in a towel, demands to be Professor Plum. A few minutes later, she reappears from behind the orange paisley curtain, damp hair knotted, dressed in fresh clothes.

Comfy jog bottoms.

Flip-flops.

And a purple T-shirt, with a yellow smiley face on the front.

"Yeah, it's new," she says, seeing my expression, and holding out the hem of the T-shirt. "Present from Catrin. You like?"

"Mm." I nod.

I do. I *will*, because it's Red's T-shirt: the one she's been wearing every single day.

Only that doesn't mean I *will* like it, not any more. Not now Red isn't the girl I'm guaranteed to be.

That's when it hits me.

If I'm not going to become Red – what happens to her?

11. THE RED DRAGON

I dream of home.

In my bedroom, the tessellating photographs have grown across my walls like slimy moss. More pictures than I could take in a year, snapshots from the future. I try to get closer, to see what's in them: to see what's coming. But the pictures turn their backs and hide.

My head stays under the pillow as I hear Tiger shift around, hunting for trainers; Mum and Dad getting up, flooding the caravan with coffee smells. I fake sleep when muffled voices offer me a cup. If I stay here with Milly, in my little cave of warmth, nothing will go wrong. Nothing will hurt. My future can't be messed up if I stay in bed instead.

I really do go back to sleep, though. It's almost eleven when I wake up. I shower, get dressed. The caravan's quiet:

a scribbled note from Dad on the table, *Gone to the shops, lazybones. See you for lunch? x.*

Merlin's coat is draped over the shoulders of a kitchen chair. I slip it on, breathing in: smoke and minty gum.

I feel like a weirdo. Is that pervy, sniffing someone's coat?

If Red were here, she'd be laughing at me. But she's not. I don't know where she's gone. I walk to the edge of the cliffs, where the iron railings lean out, groping towards Mulvey Island and the Bee rock. I take the short-cut path to the Prom, to The Bench. It's where she always goes when she's not with me, to sit and watch the tide go in, the tide go out. I always thought it was because she was waiting for something.

But she can't have been. My summer isn't her summer. She didn't have herself hissing in her own ear, telling her the future, some of it true. By being here, she had to be changing her own history.

But what does that mean for her?

What happens to her now? To the year she's already lived? To the girl who wished herself back on her fourteenth birthday?

The wind ripples the grey sea, rolling in, rolling out. It licks the pebbles, tumbling them into a new order. It washes me with sadness, as I begin to understand.

By the time I get back to the caravan park, I can smell burnt toast and there's music filtering out through the thin walls: Johnny and the Hurricanes. It's from Tiger's favourite CD. Through the windows I can see Dad twirling Tiger, while Mum drums on the table with butter knives.

Red's outside, looking in.

"I think it's called a predestination paradox," I say quietly. "Is that right?"

"Knew I could count on you to know the right technical term," she says, with a laugh like a sigh.

"It's impossible," I say, slowly, still working it all out. "I have to become you, so you can come back in time to change things. But because you've come back in time to change things, I'll never become you. Impossible."

Red shoots me a wan smile. "I recommend not thinking too hard about it. It's like the wish. I mean, how was any of this possible? Even I don't know. But here we are. Reckon you just make the best of wherever you've ended up."

"But—" I can hardly bear to look at her. "But what about you? If I don't turn into you, what happens? Where do you go?"

Red pushes her hand against the caravan wall, wisps of smoke trailing up as it disappears. Solemn, she watches her fingers as they gradually re-form into a solid hand-shape.

"Where did my hand just go? Don't know. Guess I'll just . . . stop."

"And you're OK with that? You don't mind?"

Red takes a very deep breath, and says nothing, and I think about her not taking any more deep breaths, ever; not shaking her hair over her eyes or flashing her grin or tap-tap-tapping the side of her nose. I want to hold her hand but I can't. She'll never hold anyone's hand again, ever.

"I'd mind," I say, my voice very small and choked.

Red breathes in deeply again, and sniffs. "I mind," she says, her voice small too. "I think it's all right to mind."

There's a beep-beep-beep from the smoke alarm, and the caravan door springs open, pouring out music, giggling, and the smell of charred bread. Tiger doesn't see me: she's too busy wafting a grill pan billowing grey smog out of the door at arm's length, shouting, "Water, water!" between fits of laughter.

The song changes: Link Wray, something slinky and slow. Dad whoops and cranks up the volume. Mum appears in the doorway, and empties a bowlful of water over the black toast. It sizzles, sending up more smoke. Then she takes the pan from Tiger and whips it sharply to her left, keeping tight hold of the handle, and sending the squares of black wet toast arcing into the sky.

I hear a slap-slap-slap, as they land on the roof of the chalet opposite.

"Mum!" yelps Tiger, and the two clutch each other as they stumble inside, senseless with giggles.

The door slaps closed behind them. Link Wray gets quieter, though the caravan still quivers and creaks as they dance across the crack in the curtains.

Red steps up closer, and peers in: her nose pressed as close against the glass as a wishgirl's can be.

"Hey," I say quietly, my heart aching for her; for me, when I was her. "You can come in, you know. You don't have to hide out here."

She shakes her head.

"I like watching." She sighs as Tiger dumps Dad on

129

the sofa and pulls Mum out of her seat, rock and rolling around her while she taps the beat on her belly. "I like seeing that they're all right without me."

They're not without me. I'm standing right here.

But I know what she means.

Red's a girl made of smoke, and might-have-been, things I didn't do and never will. But she was me once. *She's my mum too*, she said at the hospital. This is her family.

She's starting to say goodbye.

"I'll look after them," I whisper. "I promise."

There's a red wing of hair in the way, so I can't see her face. But she nods, and I know we understand each other.

I go inside and eat cheese on toast, version number two. I join in the dancing, Merlin's tailcoat twirling out behind me, knocking cups off the table. I let my brain tick-tick-tick.

I can't save Red, not really. I can't save her from wisping away into smoky nothingness when this summer is over – but I can follow her lead, do things her way: brave, and fabulous. That way even when she's gone, she'll still be a part of me.

And I realize: I know exactly what I need to do next.

Dad drives Mum off for her four p.m. hospital check-up.

Tiger changes her clothes, little skirt, big shoes, off to see Catrin.

I walk, and walk, the long way round, building up my courage. I go to the fairground, to face my fears.

The Shed is closed up early, for Fifties Fest preparation: boxes of hot-dog buns, a tower of stacking plastic chairs outside. I'm disappointed. I want to see Fozzie, even if I can't explain. I want Fozzie to see this.

But maybe it's something I need to do on my own.

The fairground is packed: jerky music, flashing lights, food and screaming. Chaos. Happiness. I feel it buzz through me, the rattle of the Rock'n'Roller like a bass line up my spine. My hands tingle as I weave through the crowds, feeling curious eyes on me. A girl in an oversized black tailcoat, on a sunny early evening in August. I suppose I look a little odd. I smile back, hands in Merlin's pockets. I like being a little odd, I think.

The towering iron loop of the Red Dragon looms in the sky. The plume of flame shoots in the air as the shining red carriages make the loop, and the gathered crowd gasp.

I'm not scared.

Red wouldn't be scared.

I'm not going to fall.

Red wouldn't fall.

I am Bluebell Jones, thirteen years old, and I don't need to be rescued. I can rescue myself.

The queue shuffles slowly forward as the Dragon makes its journey round the tracks, over and over. Its yellow eyes blaze, daring me to quit. It puffs out smoke, spits its flames.

I pay my money, and let them strap me in.

There's a pause, before we set off: long enough for me to wonder what the hell I was thinking and feel a stab of panic. I can see a flash of red hair in the crowd. Red is watching from below, head cocked, her mouth half-open in a curious smile as if she can't believe what she's seeing.

I cling to the safety bar over my shoulders with both hands, adjusting my grip again and again.

Then with a jolt, it starts.

I'm tipped back as we crank our way up the first slope, my regret rising notch by notch, high above the fair to linger, terrifyingly, on the brink – what have I done, *what have I done* – before we plunge, super-fast, down the first drop and then curve left, up, over and on to our sides, corkscrewing to a slow level section that suddenly drops down, twists sickeningly fast to the right and then hurls us up, up, upside-down.

We hang in time and space.

The fairground lights are tiny flashes below us, the ground impossibly far off. My forehead feels cool, my fringe dangling off it – then suddenly a shocking burst of fire shoots towards me, so fast, so close, licking at my face till I'm sure it'll singe my hair, set me alight.

But we're already moving again, out of the loop, up and around one more, gentler curve till we suddenly slow, and jerk to a stop.

I did it.

I feel sick and dizzy and I'm not sure my legs will work enough to get me out and down to the ground – but I did it. By myself. For both of us.

It feels like my birthday all over again. The one I always imagined, where I'm a butterfly. I'm not Red yet; there's so much more I need from her. But I've taken the first big step.

Red's waiting for me as I stumble queasily past the

screens showing the snap of my face: eyes wide, mouth set. Then her eyebrows lift, and her lips form a secret smile.

"Impressed?" I say, twirling.

"Hell yeah!" she says, as if she can't quite believe it. "And I'm not the only one."

She steps back, so I can see.

Merlin is leaning against Madame Soso's painted booth, watching me. He's wearing his usual magician ensemble – top hat, tight black jeans, smudgy eyeliner – but his bare arms look thin and pale, wrapping awkwardly across his chest as I approach.

"You look cold," I giggle, still giddy from the ride.

"Yeah? Some girl stole my coat," he says, smiling.

"Sorry. I didn't mean to run off with it like that, last night."

"Nonono," he says, wagging a long finger as I start to shrug it off. "Please. If you give it back now, then *you'll* be cold."

"I can't keep it. It's yours."

It's part of you, I mean: part of your Merlin-ness, like Red's wing of hair.

"True," he says. "All right, I'll make you a deal. You can give it back to me on Saturday."

"Saturday?"

"When I take you to the Fifties Fest." He coughs. "I heard there's this excellent band playing, about twelve o'clock: Joanie and the Whales, I think they're called? And, um." He coughs again. "I'm sure you're probably going anyway, like. But I thought you might come with me. We could, you know. Go together."

133

He sucks on his lower lip, hands twisting nervously.

"Oh," I say. "*Oh*. Like. Sort of. Like a date?"

Merlin coughs again, shoving his hands into his pockets. "Yeah. Sort of like a date. If that was a thing you wanted to do."

I picture the face Red must be making behind me, and giggle again.

"Yeah," I say, grinning like my face'll split while that bird flaps madly in my chest. "That's a thing I want to do."

Merlin lifts his hazel eyes up, as if to check I'm not kidding, then lets out a huge huff of breath. "Bloody hell, that was hard. Is it always that hard, asking people out?"

"No idea. But I said yes, so you must have done all right."

"Yeah," he says. "You said yes."

He just stands there, nodding and smiling, as if he's only planned up to this part, not beyond. Then he checks himself, looks at his watch, and scowls.

"I got to run. But. So. I'll meet you at The Bench, on Saturday? Just before twelve o'clock?"

I nod.

He takes one step forward, towards me, reaching out as if he's going in for a hug but thinking better of it: hesitating with his arms stiffly out like a robot. It's awkward, but adorable. He looks at my lips. My heart flaps, madly.

Then he scoops up my hand, half-lost in his coat sleeves, and presses it to his lips, keeping his eyes locked on mine.

A kiss, on the back of my hand.

I can't breathe.

His lips are still there, kissing my hand.

Then he grins, tips his hat, and he's gone, whirling into the crowd.

I stand still, trembling all over, staring at my hand.

Red stares at it too, absently rubbing a hand across the smiley face on her T-shirt as if she can feel that mad bird flapping too.

"You don't mind?" I ask, because, well, she saw him first.

She shakes her wing of hair, and flashes me her widest, reddest grin.

Dad texts: *Can you come home?*

I float back to the caravan, hardly able to walk in a straight line. Everyone's waiting: Mum on the sofa, Dad and Tiger at the table, hot chocolate in mugs for four.

Then Dad drops the bomb.

"We're leaving Penkerry. We go home first thing tomorrow."

12. OFF THE MAP

"What?" says Tiger.

"What?" I echo.

They can't mean it. Not now. Now when I've got the Red Dragon wind in my hair, when I can still feel Merlin's kiss on my hand.

Mum rearranges the duvet across the arc of her tummy, and smoothes her hands calmly across it, saying nothing.

"Seriously, what?" says Tiger again, slapping Dad's hand away from the *Fifties Fest!* flier he's folding into smaller and smaller triangles.

Hot chocolate, like a treat. They've planned this. Dad's eyes slide to Mum's in secret agreement, and the sugary smell makes me seasick.

"Listen, girls." Dad looks at his hands, big and red. "Your mum needs bed rest. And apparently bed rest does not include sitting behind a drum kit, bashing the hell out of it next to three amps and a subwoofer."

"Crazy, right?" says Mum, sweeping her hand across

her bump. "We all know Peanut here is a junior muso, just getting a head start in the school of rock. But my placenta and my cervix are having musical differences."

"The difficult third album," says Dad, mock serious. "Every band struggles with it."

"And Joanie and the Whales can't play the Fifties Fest without Joanie. And the Whales is a crappy band name."

"I still say we could be Ian and the Whales. . ." says Dad.

"But no one is ever going to pay money to see a band called Ian and the Whales. Especially not one without a drummer. I'm indispensable." Mum throws up her hands. "What can you do?"

"Shut up!" shouts Tiger. "Stop joking around, it's not funny."

It isn't, it isn't. I want to cry. This can't be real.

Mum and Dad exchange another look, and Dad sinks into his shoulders.

"You're right, it's not funny," he says, rubbing his eyes. "We're sick over it, sweetheart. Sick with worry. So disappointed. But it's a simple fact: your mum's not well. We go home tomorrow; she gets proper rest in a proper bed till Peanut comes. It's not all bad news, girls. Tiger, you'll get to pick up your exam results with all your mates. Blue, you and me'll have a laugh together. We can make a head start on all the stuff that needs doing: get the cot set up, get the painting done. . ."

"What painting?"

Mum looks at me, uncomfortable. "Don't have a paddy, baby. I thought you'd have figured this out already. After the first few weeks or months Peanut's going to need its own place to sleep—"

"And for all the million tons of crap it apparently 'needs'," says Dad, making air-quotes, "though you two did just fine without a changing table, and three kinds of sling, and a magic bucket that eats nappies. . ."

Mum ignores him. "So your bedroom's going to be the nursery."

I don't believe this. It keeps getting worse, and worse.

"Your bedroom's tiny anyway; you'll have more space once you're sharing with Tiger. You've managed in that bunk-bed cupboard together for the last few weeks. Compared to that, Tiger's room'll be like a palace."

"Do I get any say in this?" yells Tiger.

"What about all my stuff?" I whisper. The Great Mouse Army. My perfectly tessellating photos, creeping up the wall; all the new ones I'm waiting to add. The room I've got planned, to reflect me back at myself.

"It's stuff, who cares about stuff?" Dad shouts. "Are you not even listening? Are you that selfish? Your mum's not well. It's done, girls." He slaps his palm down on the table. "Grow up. Accept it."

"I don't have to accept anything!" says Tiger.

"Yes you do! This is for your mum. What kind of dad would I be if I put anything before Peanut being safe and sound, eh?"

"What kind of dad are you if you put everything else before your other kids' happiness?" says Tiger. "What if we don't want to leave?"

"None of us wants to, darling," says Mum, softly.

"Then don't! We can't go now. I can't leave now. I can't leave Catrin." Tiger's voice cracks, and she slides out from the table, turning her back.

Mum presses her lips together, head tilting. "Tiger. . ."

"I know what you're going to say," says Tiger, very slow and deliberate though her voice is still crackly. "That I'm being silly, it's just a crush, I'm a silly little girl with stupid romantic ideas and if we go home I'll forget all about her in five minutes."

My face burns. The back of my hand tingles where Merlin's lips brushed it.

"Only it's not," she says, turning around. "I love her. I do. I met her the very first night we were here, and she looked at me like she could see straight into my brain, like she knew we were going to be together, and – she's all I think about. I need her hand in mine. I need to be with her. I don't want Mum to be ill or anything bad to happen to Peanut, I don't, I swear I don't – but we've only just started and she's the most important thing that's ever happened to me and I won't let you take her away. I won't."

The bird flaps in my chest. My heart's too full with wanting. That's me, that's what I can have too, with Merlin, beautiful strange kissable Merlin – but not now. Not if we leave now. I need more time. This is too unfair. This is wrong.

Tiger shudders and runs to our bedroom, tries to slam the paisley curtain behind her, then noisily starts to weep.

Dad breathes in, breathes out.

Mum looks at me, as if she's waiting for me to fix it.

"I hate you," I whisper through a sob.

I follow Tiger, climb into my bunk with Milly Mouse, and cry-cry-cry.

I cry myself to sleep.

I dream of dragons.

They coil around my tiny bedroom, now painted blue, but not for me. I keep trying to get in but they're dragons: they can breathe fire, and I'm just a little girl.

My face hurts when I wake up.

I hear Tiger sniffle, and hang my head off the bunk.

Her face is swollen, puffy and red-raw from sobbing. Mine must be too. We look like sad clowns, and when I meet her eye I try to smile about it, but instead it makes us both start to cry again.

"God, please, girls, *stop*," says Dad, tugging back the orange curtain, sounding exhausted. "I didn't mean. . . Come and talk, will you? There's toast and tea on the table."

"No," I croak. "I don't care what you say. I'm not packing my things. I'm not leaving today. I can't."

"We're not going today," calls Mum, from the kitchenette.

I hang off the bunk again, catch Tiger's wild look of hope. We tumble out of bed in yesterday's clothes.

"That was your dad's daft idea," says Mum, pushing tea mugs across the table to us. "Make a clean break, instead of having a miserable last few days."

"Like ripping off a plaster," Dad says, defensively holding his mug up to his face.

"So we're going to stay for the Fest, tomorrow. We won't be able to play, but we can watch all the other bands. That'd give you enough time to say a proper goodbye to everyone, right? And then we'll drive back crack of dawn Sunday morning."

"When the traffic's a nightmare and half of Wales will be trying to drive down the same single-lane road as us," Dad mutters.

"So we could stay a bit longer, then?" I say, suddenly hopeful.

"Were you not listening last night?" Dad snaps. "Your mum needs rest, you think she's getting that in a caravan? We need to be *home*."

I look at Mum, feeling sick, and guilty – but Mum looks furious.

"Thank you, I can speak for myself! Don't go making out this is all my fault, I feel bad enough as it is."

I hate this. My parents don't fight. They never fight. This is all Peanut's fault.

Mum breathes deeply, stroking her round tummy with one hand, taking Dad's hand with the other.

"Ian, we've been over this. You want to stay for the Fest

as much as the rest of us, and admitting that won't make anyone think you're a bad father – just like me spending Saturday sitting on a beach in the sun won't do Peanut any harm. We drive back Sunday morning, and if we get stuck in traffic, oh well, worse things happen at sea. And that way everyone gets to have what they want."

"No we don't," says Tiger, bitterly.

"No, we don't," says Dad, and he sighs, as if he can picture another summer; one where this doesn't happen. "But it's the best we're going to get, love."

"What about my bedroom?" I ask.

"Sorry, baby." Mum shakes her head. "I can grow a person, I can't grow us a bigger house. Your dad'll go and get the paint next week."

Dad pushes back his chair and grabs his guitar, ruffling my hair like an apology. He quietly strums on the sofa, head down. End of discussion.

And that's it.

We're leaving first thing on Sunday. It's Friday morning. Two whole days.

It's not enough time. But it might have to be.

The sad, pinched look on Red's face confirms it when I find her waiting for me on the cliff top, hair blowing, looking out to sea.

"So this is one of those fixed, unchangeable stops on Bluebell Road, then?"

"You're leaving?" Red asks.

I nod. "Sunday. Same as it was for you?"

"Yeah. I thought ... maybe ... you know, you've changed so many other things. But I don't think that one was ever going to turn out different."

I could yell at her for not telling me, but there's no point. I know what she'll say: no fun without surprises. It wouldn't have changed how I've lived the last few weeks, even if I'd known. I couldn't have got to where I am any quicker.

Anyway, it's worse for her. I'm going home. I don't think she's coming with me.

"Hey – what's it like, having to share a bedroom with Tiger?"

Red half-laughs. "Oh, don't you worry. She's not so bad, our big sister, you know?"

As she speaks, she keeps her eyes on the grey waves, crashing far below. I stare across the water: to the lighthouse on Mulvey Island, the Bee rock hardly visible under the high tide; the Pavilion on the pier; the glitter of the fairground. It seems so long ago now, when we first stood here together, and I took my very first Diana photograph, of a patch of empty grass.

It knocks the air from my lungs suddenly; how much Red's done for me. She couldn't give me a perfect summer – not with Mum poorly, and bedrooms, and only two days left – but she's tried so hard. And all this time she's had to watch me do the things she never did; things she'll never do now. Without envy, or bitterness. Just to be kind, to some

143

future, past, new version of herself. I don't know if I could be that generous.

But I want to be. I don't want my Red self to disappear.

And I realize: it doesn't have to. I'm taking her with me, one way or another.

"Come on," I say, running for the short-cut path. "No time to waste."

"Where are we going?"

It's the first time she's ever had to ask.

The whole town's beginning to buzz with Fifties Fest anticipation. There's bunting between the lamp posts on the promenade; a field up on Penkerry Point roped off as a car park already, another as a second campsite. A few early arrivals are on the prom, and I get to halfway through my second roll of Diana film snapping a turquoise car with fins and creamy leather seats, crammed with big-shouldered ladies in polka dots.

I don't have time to spare, though.

First stop: the tiny Penkerry pharmacy, to buy hair dye.

Second stop: every other shop in Penkerry, because the pharmacy only does Ash Blonde and Dad's Espresso Coffee Deluxe, Guaranteed to Blend Away Greys! and I need a little more electricity.

At last, I find a bottle of wash-in, wash-out *Sonic Red* in a tiny tucked-away place that smells like patchouli.

"What are you doing?" hisses Red.

144

I look round, and spot, over her shoulder, the neon sign:
EAR-PIERCING AVAILABLE

My stomach turns over, but I can't ignore it. It's as if the universe guided me here, and is speeding me down my road towards Red.

"Blue, wait, are you sure. . .?" says Red, as I poke through my purse.

The last of my birthday money is enough to cover it. One bottle of hair dye, and two fat gold studs, throbbing painfully in my ear.

"What are you doing with those scissors?"

"Nothing," I tell Mum, slicing the leg off my favourite jeans.

The other follows, snip-snip-snip. I slip them on. Not straight. One leg's longer than the other. I don't have time or money for the biker boots, but it's a start.

"I'm just going to borrow your T-shirt, Tiger, OK?"

I poke at the clothes mountain on the floor.

"No chance," Tiger calls back from the bathroom, where she's soaking the redness from her eyes. "I'm never lending you anything ever again, not after you lost my best ever, most beloved favourite scarf."

I can't argue that. Who knows where it ended up. There's probably a starfish somewhere at the bottom of the sea using it as a house. I start excavating through the layers of socks, Austen novels and headphones anyway.

Tiger swishes through the curtain in a smog of her favourite perfume. White-blonde dreadlocks, vast blue eyes – and a scruffy purple T-shirt, with a smiley yellow face.

She catches me staring, and smirks.

"Duh! *Catrin* gave me this. I'm probably never taking it off again."

She crosses her arms across her chest, firmly.

No T-shirt. No boots. But it's OK. I can compromise on a few details, so long as I get the big stuff right.

"I need you to cut my hair."

I hold out the scissors, handle first. Tiger is the family hairdresser: has been for as long as I remember. I hope I can describe the parakeet wing over one eye right. It's not like I can show her a photo.

"I'm going out," she says crossly, grabbing her bag and stepping over me.

"You can't! I need you to do this first!"

I contemplate the scissors, wondering if I could just chop the ponytail off myself, all in one go. Is that how Red did it?

"Can't you at least help me dye it?"

"Dye it?" Mum pokes her head through the curtain, as Tiger swishes out. "Don't think so, baby. I've already had an earful about the stains in the bathroom. Wait till we get home, then it's only our sink you'll be buggering up. And our towels. And our carpet. Yeah, maybe you can't do it when we get home either."

She plucks the bottle of wash-in dye from my hand, and eyes me. "*Sonic Red*? Seriously?"

"Mum!"

"I don't want you mucking about with your beautiful hair, sweetie," she says, combing her fingers through my stupid ponytail. Then she gasps. "Oh my god, what did you do to your ear?"

"Nothing," I say, jerking my head away. "It's pierced. Don't yell at me."

"Who's yelling?" Mum frowns, squeezing my arm. "I don't mind you having your ear pierced, baby – though I'd rather you'd told me, before. But you definitely don't want to do your hair now. You need to keep the piercing clean, you don't want to get dye in it."

I shake her off. "It's not up to you. It's my ear. It's my hair."

I push past her to the bathroom. I pull out my ponytail, and start rearranging it in the mirror, brushing out a too-long wing to sweep across one eye, pinning up the back. Not Red, not right, but closer.

Dad groans from the sofa. "Please tell me Peanut isn't going to grow up to be a teenager?"

"Sorry, love. Looks like we're two for two so far."

They laugh together, as if they think they're so so funny; as if all of this panic and rush isn't their fault.

I pull on Merlin's coat, grab the bottle of dye, and slam the caravan door behind me.

"What are you doing?" says Red, face crunched as she looks at my new halfway hairdo.

She's been waiting outside, listening in.

"No time," I say.

147

It's not her I need right now. I want to go straight to Merlin's, spend every last second I can with him – but I want it to be perfect when I see him. I've got a picture in my head: exactly how it should be. For that I need Fozzie. She'll understand why I need to dye my hair, today, right now, without me needing to explain anything. I can't wait to tell her about the hand-kissing. She'll lend me some fabulous clothes; better than a T-shirt. She'll show me how to do my face all painted and perfect. We can have a girly teenage talk about boys. I've never had one of those, and now I need one. Urgently. With instructions.

I breathe in the spearminty smell all around me, and break into a run.

The Shed is in chaos; a van parked outside, crammed with boxes of crisps and ice-cream cones. Inside I can see Dan and Mags, sweating over a new table, puzzling out how to fit it together. I peer hopefully past them, but I can't see Merlin.

Fozzie rounds the van carrying a huge bag of paper cups, and nearly walks right through me.

"Oh!" She doesn't give me her usual smile. She's not like herself at all: hair scraped back, face pink from the effort. "Hi. 'Scuse me."

"Sorry!" I step back, as she dump the box, and collects another from behind the van. "You look really busy."

"I am," she says, hefting the box, sliding it on to the

other. "I'd have asked you to come down and help, but, well, I haven't seen you, have I?"

"I'm sorry!" I start helping her take bags out of the van, but she snatches them angrily from my hands. "I had to. . . Something came up."

"Let me guess: you had to go off to hang out with that other special friend of yours? Guess you two worked out your issues. Jason, who runs the Red Dragon now? He says you were down here last night having a whale of a time."

"I did look for you," I say feebly. I don't know why she's so cross. She's got other friends too.

Dan bangs out of The Shed, his usual cheery grin fading right off his face the moment he sees me.

"All right, Foz?" he says, rolling up his sleeves.

She gives him a grim nod.

"Hi, Dan," I say.

He hefts two bags on to his shoulders and goes back inside without a word; only a dismissive shake of his head.

This is awful. This isn't how this is meant to go at all.

"Is that Merlin's coat?" Fozzie crinkles her nose, critically.

A smile sneaks on to my face. I can't help it. I'm longing to see him. Like that wait in a restaurant when you've ordered lasagne, and they bring out other people's plates first, hot and delicious-smelling, and all you can think is *lasagnelasagnelasagne* till you can almost taste it on your tongue.

This is how much I need a girly chat with someone who knows what they're doing: I think boys are like lasagne.

"Yes! Foz, I've got so much to tell you. You won't believe it. Unless – is he here?" I ask, peering into The Shed.

"Yeah, right, like he'd actually turn up when he says he will." She narrows her eyes. "Is that the only reason you're here? To find Merlin?"

"No," I say, in a voice that means yes. "No! I wanted to – look, I need you to help me. We're going on a date! And I've got hair dye. Because – see – all this stuff has happened, and. . . Can we go and just, you know, hang out?"

I want her to smile at me, and tell me about some weird film I've never heard of that will teach me about dating. I want to sit in her bedroom, waiting for my hair to turn cherry red. I want her to stop looking at me like I've broken something.

"I'm busy."

She grabs two huge plastic sacks of popcorn and hauls them towards the doors.

"Wait! That's not the only thing I came to tell you. We're leaving. We're not staying for the rest of the summer. We're leaving this weekend."

"Oh!" she says, honest disappointment sneaking into her eyes before she can hide it. "Right. I heard they were changing the band line-up, getting someone else in to open the Fest."

"Yeah. Mum's not well enough to play. We're going to stay to watch, but we'll be off Sunday morning."

"She OK, your mum?"

I nod, and she nods back, once, sharp.

150

"Give her my best."

"I will."

We stand there.

"Nothing else you want to say?" Fozzie says, tapping her foot, her mouth a flat line of annoyance.

Why's she being like this? She should be hugging me, telling me she'll miss me, demanding we spend every last second together.

"Is this because of Merlin? Are you . . . *jealous?*"

Fozzie groans out loud. "Jealous? You are having a laugh. Can't believe you even think that. But then you're not the girl I thought you were, are you?"

She wheels inside with the popcorn.

A few seconds later, she marches back out and thrusts a parcel into my hands, wrapped in shiny gold paper.

"What's this?"

"Your birthday present. The one I was going to give you at your birthday party in the Cave. You remember that? The party I organized for you? The one you ran out of in tears, without a word of explanation, and never even said thank you?"

She presses her lips together, her face burning.

"I'm so sorry," I mumble. I feel terrible.

"No, it's fine. You've got this other friend, who treats you like crap and upsets you, drags you away from your mates – you know, the people who actually like you. But it's fine that she's the one you want to hang with. Her, Merlin, whoever. I mean, I think we would've had a laugh if we'd hung out more – but, hey, not my choice. It'll be

151

jammed in here for the Fest tomorrow; don't know if I'll see you again. So, here you go. Call it a leaving present."

She folds her arms, tilting her head at the present expectantly.

Guiltily, I peel back the wrapping paper.

Rebel Without A Cause, on DVD. Her favourite.

"We could go and watch this, together?" I say, hopefully. "Right now. We can go to your room, and while it's on you can dye my hair, and lend me earrings, and. . ."

Fozzie sighs and picks up another two sacks of popcorn.

"Have a nice life, Blue."

She goes back inside.

Mags slams the Shed door shut behind her, glares at me through the window, and flips the sign over, hard.

Closed.

13. MERLIN

"What the hell are you doing?"

Red is standing outside Madame Soso's, feet planted.

"Go back in there!" she shouts, jabbing a finger at The Shed. "That was your chance to make things up with her, do you not get that? You might not get another."

I scratch my fingernail into the plastic of the DVD box.

"So? I'm leaving anyway, it's not like it makes any difference."

I don't mean it. Everything Fozzie said is sitting in my stomach, rolling over.

But Red won't stop. "You don't get any of this, do you? This was your second chance. *My* second chance. Do you know how many people get one of those? Do you know how many people would kill for one? And what do you do with it? You yell at Mum and Dad like a spoiled brat, treat Tiger's stuff like rubbish. You run around making friends and having a laugh and not caring, not even noticing when you let them down. Did you never think Fozzie might have been hurt that you ran off from the party? You didn't even thank her for the leaving present!"

I shake my overlong wing of hair off my face, flash my eyes, not caring that we're in the middle of the fair and I'm yelling at air.

"That's not my fault! *You* made me leave the party. You lied. Everything that's gone wrong is your fault!"

"How is it *my* fault?"

"Because I'm running out of time! I'm supposed to be a butterfly when we go. I can't go home still being stupid Bluebell who collects toy mice. I need to do it all before we leave: my hair, the earrings, the boots. . ."

Red starts back like she's been stung.

"You really think that's what this was all about – a haircut and a pair of shoes? You know what really proves you've grown up? *Acting* grown up. Caring about other people instead of just yourself. Taking some responsibility. Thinking about the consequences of your actions. Choosing what kind of person you'd like to be. Trying to be a better one."

"I am doing all those things!"

"You're not." She stares at me, her face crumpling. "I thought this time around I could at least get some of it right. Blue was a nice girl, you know. There was nothing wrong with who you were."

"What would you know, you're not even real!" I can't believe how nasty my voice sounds, but she's hurting me: I want to hurt her back. "You're only here because I wished you here – and the only reason you're saying any of this is because I'm replacing you. Because I'm better at this than you are!"

"I thought you understood." She shakes her head, bewildered. "I thought I'd said too much. Thought you'd see it coming a mile away. But you haven't heard a thing, have you?"

She turns and walks away.

"Fine! Go! I don't need lessons from you!"

She halts, hesitating before she looks over her shoulder.

"If that's true, Bluebell," she says, her eyes tracking across my pinned-up hair, my ragged cut-offs. "Why are you trying so hard to be me?"

The hill up to the far side of town is steep, but fury powers me up. I can't believe everyone is ruining my last few days in Penkerry like this. Even Red. She's meant to be on my side. You can't trust anybody.

Merlin will understand, though. He's like me: different. Dissatisfied. And special, as well. Magical.

I pick out his huge white house from the row looking out over the bay, and step through the gate to ring the bell. It's not as white as it looks, close up. The paint is flaking away, and there's some sort of grey mossy stuff growing over it. The paint on the door's flaking off, too.

There's a long wait, so I ring again.

Eventually the door opens a crack, and half of Merlin's

face appears. My chest feels tight, just seeing the shadow of his cheekbone, one hazel eye. No eyeliner today. Without it, he looks sleepy and clean.

"Hello?" He blinks a few times. "Oh. Blue. I thought we were meeting tomorrow, at The Bench?"

"We are." My smile is automatic. "But – I sort of needed to see you now. Can I come in?"

He frowns, peering over his shoulder. "Uh. . ."

"Who's at the door?" says a woman's voice. "Who's at the door?"

I hear shushing, then the door is pulled open fully.

"Excuse my son's manners," says a tall grey-haired man in a buttoned-up waistcoat, shirt and tie. He looks more like Merlin's grandfather than his dad.

Merlin, now I can see all of him, looks like someone else entirely. It's not just the lack of eyeliner. He's wearing flappy shorts and a red nylon football shirt, his hair flat and hatless. He looks as shocked as I feel.

"Come in, dear," says Merlin's dad, leading the way down a carpeted hall.

There are lots of doors. There's a smell, too: like bins, and wee. Maybe they've got a cat.

I follow them into a huge kitchen. Merlin's dad sits down to ruffle a newspaper. Merlin just stands there in his shiny shirt, awkward.

The smell's stronger in here. There's food everywhere: used pans on the stove, empty Pop-Tart boxes left by the toaster – and things, in piles, stacked against the walls: more newspapers, crockery, plastic tubs with tiny

156

cardboard boxes inside. It's like someone forgot to tidy up, for about a year.

"So," Merlin says, shuffling his feet. "You ... you needed something?"

My eyes shift over to his dad behind the newspaper. I want to go to another room. Talk to him properly. Have him hold my hand, and be magical again.

"We're leaving. I'm leaving. On Sunday. So I'm only here today, and tomorrow."

His face falls. He swallows. Jerks a hand out towards me. Pulls it back, self-conscious, eyes straying across the room to his dad. Puts his hand out again.

I lift mine too and our fingers weave together, a knot. His fingerprints press against my bones. His thumb strokes my palm.

"Gareth? *Gareth?*"

It's the woman's voice again, very quavery.

Merlin's face closes up.

I expect the old man to go, but Merlin slips his hand from mine and darts out into the hallway.

"It's OK, Mum, I'm coming," he calls.

His dad goes on reading the paper, chewing on a sandwich.

I don't know if I'm supposed to stay, or follow Merlin. The smell and the stillness start to stick to me, greasy and sad.

"My wife has early onset Alzheimer's disease," announces the old man, not looking up from his newspaper. "It means she has dementia. Do you understand?"

We did a project on grandparents in primary school. Harry Parker's gran had dementia. She had to go into a home.

I nod, then realize he's not looking at me. "Yes. It means you forget things."

"It means other things too," he says heavily, putting down the paper and clasping his hands on the table. "But yes. You forget things. First the small ones, like where you've left your handbag. Then the words for things: people included. Then the things themselves. Finally yourself."

He says it like facts, like what's on TV. He doesn't look upset, or angry. I suppose those things pass.

"Is that why she called Merlin Gareth, just then? She's forgotten his real name?"

Merlin's dad purses his lips disapprovingly.

"Gareth is his real name. 'Merlin' is an affectation we don't tolerate in this house – much like that costume he so likes to wear." He nods at me: at the tailcoat I'm still wearing. He picks up the paper, shaking it out. "It confuses her, you see."

I grip the too-long sleeves, drawing the coat around me.

He keeps reading, and I slip out, back down the hallway.

There's an open door. I can hear Merlin – Gareth – softly reading from a magazine to a pale woman in a high-backed armchair. She's about the same age as my mum. With curly dark hair, and fluffy pink slippers that aren't quite on her feet.

Merlin's head tilts up, his neck red in patches, clearly having overheard.

"Sorry," I whisper.

I don't know what else to say.

He nods, slowly.

I slip the coat off my shoulders, wanting to give it back to him, all of it. Merlin the Magician. The life I thought he had. The coat sags on the doorknob, tails trailing on the floor.

"Will you be there, tomorrow?" he asks, his voice soft but urgent.

"Of course I will. Yes. You?"

"Do my best," he says, his smile weak.

I want to say goodbye to his mum, but she's looking at Merlin, watching his lips move.

He smiles down at her, and starts reading the magazine again.

I linger at the front door, listening to the low purr of his voice reading about beauty surveys and skincare regimes. Then I let myself out.

Outside it's all blue skies, bright and fresh.

It feels obscene. The sun warms my skin, as if nothing is wrong.

Behind the peeling white front door, everything is wrong.

I'm wrong.

I thought I knew him but I don't. I thought he was special – but he's not. He's an ordinary boy with a too-real life, who wants the world to think he's a butterfly.

I can't blame him. I can't imagine how awful it must be. The blank, black space left where she should be.

So he puts on a costume, to paste over it. And I think suddenly that we're all doing it: showing the world something not quite honest. Purple boots and retro shades. Yoga bottoms and third eyes. Black dye to cover up the greys onstage. A brave face for baby. We can't help ourselves.

Maybe it is honest, after all. Nothing's hidden. We show to the world our intimate hopes, our longed-for dreams. Our better selves. There's not much more personal than that.

But the end of the day Merlin the Magician still has to go home, wipe his face clean, and be Gareth again.

My hands are shaking. I busy them in my bag, knuckling the bottle of hair dye aside, ashamed. I find Diana instead, her chunky plastic reassuring under my fingers. The process is comforting and familiar: line up, focus, wind on. I snap off a series of shots, click click click.

Here's where I took a photograph. Here's where I took a photograph. Here's where I took a photograph.

That's what Merlin said, in the Cave: that I was wasting my time. The sky is big and cloudless, an expanse of blue above an endless glittering sea, impossible to cram into the viewfinder. Not the fairground swirl of music and screams. Not salt, chips, fresh air and sugar on the wind. Not tears on my face, for everything I've got wrong. For Merlin.

I'm taking pictures, not memories. But the pictures will remind me, for ever, of how huge and strange and tragic this moment is. I *can* remember it. I didn't know how important that was.

How lucky I am.
I put the camera away and do nothing but look.
I am a camera. I see, and remember.
I think: I don't want to be anyone else.
I'm ready to be me.

14. WISHGIRL

On Saturday, Red's not the only time-traveller in town.

The extra campground in the field on Penkerry Point is rammed. There are jeans with turn-ups and cigarette packs tucked into T-shirt sleeves wherever you turn. Red lips and tight sweaters, high ponytails and hairspray-stiff fringes. The Fifties Fest crowd mingles with the usual Penkerry day trippers: trainers and smartphones, mopeds and bobby socks. It's as if all the rules of time have been wished away.

I'm not wasting one second.

It hasn't been easy. I've had to ask strangers for favours: not very Blue. I've had to admit I've been wrong, even to myself. Red was kinder than I expected. She even helped; whispered a few cheating secrets in my ear so I could make this perfect. She looked guilty. I'm guilty too. I didn't tell her about Merlin. Let her keep him as he is in her mind: a perfect dream of a boy.

There's more to do. But everything's ready.

I spend the morning packing. We won't be back to the caravan until late, and Dad wants the suitcases in a line, ready to sling in the car tomorrow. Tiger scoops her stuff off the floor in armfuls, finished in minutes. Mine takes longer, all folded. Everything fits neatly, the way I like it, unapologetically. Milly. My bluebell perfume. The photos pinned above my bunk: Peanut's scan, the patch of grass, my top-hat silhouette.

The top hat means something else now. Something sad.

Everything today is sad.

And more.

I stroke my thumb down the back of my hand, just once.

"Tea!" shouts Mum.

She's lying in state on the sofa, under instruction not to move an inch.

"I'll pack it now, all right?" I say, dragging my case out through the curtain.

"Don't pack it, make it!" she says, flapping an arm feebly.

"Milking it," says Tiger, in a sing-song voice from the kitchenette table.

"Am not!"

"Are too," calls Dad, from their bedroom.

It feels fragile. We're not quite ourselves. All on tiptoe, not sure when a joke might make someone cry instead of laugh.

I fill up the kettle, and clear out the fridge while I'm

there, pulling down the list of possible Peanut names to take with us.

"What about Lemon?" says Tiger. "Or Chive Blossom?"

"For a boy or a girl?" says Mum.

"It's not a name, it's a paint colour," Tiger snorts, flapping a booklet at her. It's a paint sampler: rows of coloured squares, all with daft names so you can tell between the seventeen shades of white.

Mum levers her head off the sofa, surprised. Dad pokes a curious head out of their room. I duck my head, embarrassed by all the drama.

"We talked, me and Tiger. Sorry about before. Peanut can have my bedroom. I *want* Peanut to have my bedroom – but on one condition. We get to pick the new paint colour."

Dad blinks, then breaks into a grin. "OK, deal. So long as you pick something, you know. Baby-friendly."

"Oi!" Mum pouts. "I'm growing a rock'n'roll superstar in here. Rock'n'roll is not pastel. You go for it, girls."

Tiger begins gleefully circling the ugliest squares of colour.

Aubergine Frenzy. Tangerine Dream. I add a few more to Peanut's name list. Mum beckons me over, and I half expect her to cross them all out again – but instead she gives me a kiss on the cheek.

She strokes my hair; fusses at my sore ear. I kiss her tummy through her top, still on tiptoe: safer than words.

"Hey, can we paint my room, too?" Tiger says, sucking the pen. "I mean, if it's going to be *our* room."

She's wearing the purple smiley-face T-shirt again, as promised; sees me eye it wistfully. She fixes her giant blue eyes on me like an offer, a hand held out.

"Make me a cup of tea and you can paint the whole bloody house," says Mum.

I fetch mugs.

Scarlet Sunset. Crimson Dream. Firecracker. Dragonskin.

The beach is packed. It's another beautiful blue-skied day: the best yet. The tide's highish, so every pebble of beach is taken. One side of the pier is all families with deckchairs and parasols, sun tents and coolers stuffed with ice. On the other side is another crowd, up on its feet, ready. Dan's easy to spot, wearing a huge inflatable doughnut to advertise the stall in the fair. Down on the pier itself, at the furthest end, there's a stage with a canopy, like a miniature rock festival hovering above the water.

The stage is empty but it's nearly twelve. Almost time for King Biscuit and the Crunchy Frogs, a scratch band made up of Woody, and Janice, and last-minute volunteers from the other line-ups. The new opening act of the Fifties Fest.

It should be Joanie and the Whales out there.

Mum and Dad's faces say they're thinking it, too. It breaks my heart. Here we all are in the sun, not feeling it. Today is all about regret.

But they hold hands, and Dad shouts, "Preggo lady

coming through!" as Mum gingerly takes the steps down on to the beach. A path clears for them, and she picks her way slowly through the chairs and sunburnt people to claim a spot on the beach, waving back at us so we can find them later.

Tiger spots Catrin and runs to her, holding her tight, not letting go.

I go to The Bench.

Red wouldn't come in, last night. I guessed she wanted to spend our last night watching the sea and the sun coming up; expected to find her waiting for me, right here. But she said I'd know where to find her today. She'll be here somewhere.

I wait, Diana in my hands, taking shot after shot of the party all around me. Trying to soak all my feelings into the film, all my sorrow and disappointment, all my hope and love.

Then there he is.

Merlin: in top hat and tails, eyeliner restored.

He hesitates as I stand up to say hi. We do an awkward dance, not sure of each other. In the end he finds his most charming smile, flicking his hat off to tumble down his arm, catching it perfectly as he sketches a deep bow.

Merlin the Magician, at my service.

It makes me sad, beautiful as he is. It's like my photographs. I can see what's not in the picture.

He straightens, and stands stiffly, clutching his hat. All nerves. Not magic at all.

I can't bear it. I grab the hat from his hands, and plonk

it on to his head. He laughs, and tips it up, and I can't help myself. I hug him. I slide my arms under his jacket. He breathes in, sharply. Then he wraps his arms across my back, tentative, then holding me close. I rest my cheek on his T-shirt.

There are hammers in there, thumping through his skin.

A wolf-whistle pierces the air, above the low thump of the music.

It's Mum, installed on a sunlounger, fingers at the corners of her mouth. Beside her I spot Dad with his shirt off, giving me two approving thumbs up.

"And let's go," I say, pushing him up the promenade with my face glowing madly.

We fall into step, Merlin's arm sliding across my shoulders.

"Hey," I mumble, suddenly struck with guilt. "I'm so sorry. About your mum."

"Thank you."

I look up, about to say more, but he shakes his head.

No need to explain.

He grabs my hand and we run along the prom, down the beach steps, into the crowd as a roar goes up and the band begin to play. The drumbeats echo off the cliffs, across the water. The crowd seethes and pulses, sweaty bodies all around me, Merlin behind me, holding me up. I get lost in the music. We get lost together.

Three bands later, we crawl through the crowd. I'm sweaty and disgusting, but so is Merlin, and he doesn't seem to mind. We get ice creams in tubs and meander down the prom, talking about nothing. Everything. Every word matters.

Over on the calmer side of the beach, the deckchairs are now all tilted back, away from the sea. There's a projector fixed to the Pavilion, playing films across the cliff face as if it's a screen. People are going round with buckets, handing out special headphone sets you can rent for two quid – but the soundless version is pretty entertaining. It's the end of one of the *Pirates* films: flashing swords and big hats. This side of the cliffs is in shade, though the sunlight's too bright for it to really work yet. Once it gets darker, it's going to look amazing.

I'm counting on it.

We weave through the deckchairs and parasols till we find our spot. Tiger and Catrin are already there on the picnic blanket, clinging. I slip in between Mum and Dad, to sit with my head resting against Mum's knee. Merlin folds his legs up like a dead spider.

Toy Story starts to play and we idly watch the familiar scenes, half of us with headphones, half making up new dialogue as we go along. I snap a few shots of the rock-lumpy faces playing across the cliff. We all take turns to wear Merlin's hat.

In the next break, Dad fetches fish and chips. Me and Merlin share.

The crowd starts to thin out, as the day trippers leave. I hate watching them go. Time's ticking away – but I don't want to waste what there is of it feeling sad.

Light flickers across the cliffs, as the next film begins.

"What's this? Isn't the next one supposed to be some sci-fi thing? Oh, wait, this is better."

Dad claps and whistles as the title appears.

Rebel Without A Cause.

I hear a whoop from further along the beach.

"Back in a sec," I whisper to Merlin, as Catrin goes off to fetch more headphones.

Dan's inflatable doughnut guides me across the pebbles, and I find him, Mags, and a mouth-open Fozzie perched on an abandoned blanket.

"Was this you?" Fozzie breathes up at me, dazed, tugging off her headphones.

"I had some help." I smile, grateful, at Mags and Dan as Fozzie stares, astonished. "Mags sweet-talked your mum into letting you leave The Shed early, so you'd get here in time. And Dan knew who to talk to in the Pavilion, to get the discs switched."

I glance up at the cliff: giant James Dean, taller than the Red Dragon.

"You did say it looked better on the big screen." I shuffle closer. "I wanted to say sorry. For everything. I didn't mean to be a rubbish friend. I wish we'd spent more time together, and I'm really going to miss you."

"Awwww, get you two," yells Dan, leaning in to give us a plasticky hug.

"You, she's not going to miss," says Mags, batting his arm away.

Dan does a fake hurt look.

"All of you. But not yet. Come on. We've got chips. And Merlin."

We snatch extra deckchairs out of the jaws of the incoming tide and expand our little camp as, slowly, the beach gets emptier. Dad and Fozzie both shout out the famous bits of dialogue. Mum and Dan have a friendly argument over which one of them is more uncomfortable – until Mum plucks the valve of his doughnut suit open, deflating him. I snap a shot of her victory cheer, and Dan, terrifyingly pasty in his Welsh dragon boxer shorts. I snap Tiger and Catrin, both gazing at the screen, expressions identical; Mags, falling asleep with an ice cream just slipping from her grasp; Fozzie frowning with concentration as Dad tries to show her how to play some particular chord on an imaginary guitar; Merlin, in close-up, looking directly into the lens; Mum, watching unobserved, quiet, happy.

They'll be sad pictures too, because they're the end of things. But they're going to radiate happy all across my new bedroom wall.

I squint at Diana in the dark, and find I've got one shot left on my last roll of film.

I look around again for Red. She won't show up in the print, but she should be here. This is her farewell party.

But there's something else I shouldn't leave behind without at least trying to capture it. One last perfect Penkerry picture.

They're all still watching the film, so I whisper to Mum that I'll be back soon, and slip away in the dark.

The pebbles are slippery and skiddy under my feet and

a few times my flowery shoes get caught by an unexpected wave, but the flickery film light projected across the cliffs is enough to see by. The lighthouse spins across the water, slow then suddenly bright, and I can see the lights of the caravan park up on the top of the Point. But I cut straight past the end of the short-cut path, lit up as the lighthouse beam tracks across. I skid on across the pebbles, listening to the waves crash, always louder at night, on and up and then down into the dip in the pebbles, and into the chill of the Cave.

I shiver, wishing there was a campfire and Verushka/Danushka playing guitar this time; candles and birthday cake.

I hold my phone up. There's no signal, but the screen light glows off the slimy walls, helping me find my way back, far back. I let the screen light travel up the algae like the lighthouse beam and there it is, high on the wall; fading already, half washed away. HAPPY BIRTHDAY BLUE, in white painted letters.

I climb up the big boulder at the back, careful not to slip, and hold up Diana with both hands. I can't use the viewfinder so I can only line up the shot, hope, and click. For all I know my final picture of Penkerry will be a wall of slime. But I'll always know what it was meant to be.

I wind the camera on, carefully slip her back into my bag, and climb down the boulder, my feet splishing into a chilly puddle as I drop.

My screen light tracks across the darkness, then catches on a face.

Red.

She's standing near the cave entrance, looking at her hands.

"Hey!" I say, relieved to have company in the dark. "Was wondering where you were. Should've known you'd go to the same place I did."

She nods, slow, deliberate. "I was always going to come here tonight. One of those big unchangeable facts that even a wishgirl can't mess with."

"Right," I say. "Did you see the film, up on the cliffs?"

She nods, smiling tightly. "Yeah. You did really well, putting everything right. You did it beautifully."

Her voice cracks, and she dips her head in the dark.

"Oh, *Red*, don't." I dart forward, wishing I could hug her: hold her hand, even. I haven't forgotten. The end of my Penkerry summer is the end of her. She'll disappear, for ever. "I'm sorry. I don't want you to go. I wish you could stay."

I wonder for a second if wishing it might be enough. It's not my birthday, but they do come true, sometimes.

"I wish Red can stay!" I say, the words echoing back at me, fading to nothing.

Red keeps her head lowered, her wing of hair flickering green in the odd light.

"Blue, I've got to tell you something."

I wait, listening to the drip-drip-plink from the cave roof.

"I'm not really here because of a birthday wish," she says, very quietly. "I'm not the fourteen-year-old you. There is no fourteen-year-old you."

172

Drip drip plink. Drip drip plink.

"That doesn't make any sense," I say, holding my phone up closer to her face, so I can see her grin flash, and laugh the eeriness away.

"I knew you'd come here, because I did too," she says, not grinning, not laughing. "I didn't know about the Cave; didn't know to check the stripes on the Bee rock outside. I wandered off from the crowds at the Fest. I found the cave and came inside. I had a look around, but when I wanted to go it was too late. The tide was too far in."

"What happened?"

"I died, Blue," she says softly. "I drowned."

I stiffen, breathing in.

Water flows over the pebbles behind her, a single wave trickling down and washing over her feet. They melt away into wisps of smoke, as if she isn't there at all.

I see it, now.

What she is.

Not a wishgirl. A ghost. The ghost of the girl I wanted to be.

"You couldn't get out of the cave?" I say, my voice small in the big space.

She gives a tiny shake of her head.

I stand very still.

"Can I get out of the cave?"

Another tiny shake.

"Am going to die?" I whisper.

My hand's shaking too much to hold up the phone, and I can't see Red's face.

She doesn't say anything. She doesn't need to.

"No," I murmur, starting forward. "No, there's got to be a way – if I know now, I can stop it—"

"It's too late. This is a tidal cave. Once the tide reaches a certain point, not even an Olympic swimmer could get themselves out. You were dead the moment you walked in here."

I shiver, hearing her say it so blankly. As if she accepts it.

"Why didn't you tell me?"

"How do you tell someone they're going to die in a few weeks?" Her voice bounces off the cave walls, echoing around us as the drips begin to splash into puddles on the ground. "No one would want to know that, before. I wouldn't have."

"I would!"

"No, Blue, you wouldn't." She steps closer, her ankles disappearing into wispy smoke again. "Think about it. If I'd told you, you'd have had a more miserable summer than I did – and where would be the point in me being here? This way's better. Short sharp shock."

"Like ripping off a plaster," I whisper numbly.

"Yeah."

"Ripping off a plaster hurts."

"I know it does, Blue. But not for long."

I look at her pale little face, and remember she's done this before.

"Where will we go?" I say, as the dip in the pebbles outside begins to crumble away, and water starts to pour into the cave. I shriek and stumble back as the cold swirls round my legs, rising, rising, so fast, so strong, trying to sweep my feet from under me.

"I don't know," she says, running her hand through the dark water, letting it dissolve into coils of smoky nothing. "Sorry. That's not a lie. I don't remember, I don't know where I came from. I don't think we get to know."

I stumble again, bumping against the boulder I climbed.

"Peanut," I say suddenly. "Is Peanut a boy or a girl?"

Red shakes her head. "I don't know. I never knew. I . . . we won't be around to find out."

"That's really sad," I say, my voice thick and strange and it's obvious, so obvious it doesn't need to be said out loud here in the dark but it is. It's really sad.

"I mind too," Red says quietly. "I think it's all right to mind."

She reaches for my hand, and when I touch her fingers, they don't disappear.

I keep holding her hand, tight tight tight, all the way down.

It will be a cold November day when they come back: a father, a sister, a mother carrying a new baby.

They will meet with a cluster of friends and stand at the end of Penkerry Pier in wind and rain, to throw flowers on the water. Not bluebells: sunflowers, bold and bright and happy. They will cry.

The father will close his eyes and – privately – wish that she'd had just a little more time: enough to keep a secret, fall in love, grow up.

The sister will – telling no one – wish they had never fought: that she'd lent her that cheap purple T-shirt with the smiley face logo.

The mother will wish that when she died, she wasn't alone.

After, they will pin the glowing girl in the top hat to every wall, every surface, to their skin, for ever. Each of them will fill in her empty silhouette in their own way, but it will always be a beautiful picture.

Violet
Poppy
~~Rose~~ OLD LADY NAME
ROSIE
Hydrangea
~~MILK THISTLE~~
Aquamarinea
MYFANWY
Angharad
Llanfairpwllgwyngyllgogerychwyrndrobllllant
isiliogogogoch (Gwyn for short)

Li (jasmine)
MEI (Plum Blossom)
LAN (Orchid Flower)
Chive Blossom
Honey Beam
Sage
Bracken
Rowan
Ash
Iolo ← ? This looks like Maths

Slate Mist
FROSTY GLEN
Ocean Spirit

APPLE
~~HEDGE~~
~~Shrub~~
~~Wicker Basket~~
Grey

flint
Song (Pine)
Hu (Tiger!)
John
WHO WROTE THIS?
Ieuan
IESTYN

ACKNOWLEDGEMENTS

This book needed to be rescued, several times over. My gratitude to Florence + the Machine and the creators of Midget Gems for keeping me at my desk through the lumpy bits, and to my nephew Dave for telling me to watch a film I can't name without spoiling it horribly. Cheers, Dave!

Big love to fellow Oxford kidlit folks Pita, Sally and Jo, for coffee, hugs and thinking; far-flung but much-beloved writing friends Sarah, Ruth, Josie and Caroline, for fixing broken things (me included); Keris, Luisa, Keren, Cat, Tamsyn, Sophia for sanity and giggles; and to the Girls Heart Books authors and readers, who make me smile every single day.

Huge thanks to my agent Caroline Walsh, for cheerfully continuing to believe in me even when I'm rubbish. Thank you to all at Scholastic – Anna, Jamie, Alyx, Lisa, and all the behind-the-scenes lovelies. Above all, my thanks to my wonderful editor Marion Lloyd, for her remarkable patience and insight, and for not letting me off my own hook.

DON'T MISS ANOTHER GREAT TITLE BY SUSIE DAY

"Thoroughly entertaining, touching and funny"
Chicklish

"Great fun ... a real romp"
Bookbag

Heidi's new boyfriend is dreamy.

Gorgeous Ed writes loving emails, rides a motorbike, and doesn't exist. He's just an online creation invented by Heidi.
Now all her friends are writing to him with their problems. Ed gives great advice — but Heidi's getting tangled up in a web of embarrassing secrets.
Her crazy double life is heading for disaster...

PREVIOUSLY PUBLISHED AS *GIRL MEETS CAKE*